D0209724

Also by Josephine Cameron

Maybe a Mermaid
A Dog-Friendly Town

NOT ALL HEROES

Josephine Cameron

Farrar Straus Giroux

New York

Farrar Straus Giroux Books for Young Readers
An imprint of Macmillan Publishing Group, LLC
120 Broadway, New York, NY 10271
mackids.com

Copyright © 2021 by Josephine Cameron
All rights reserved.

Our books may be purchased in bulk for promotional, educational, or business use. Please contact your local bookseller or the Macmillan Corporate and Premium Sales Department at (800) 221-7945 ext. 5442 or by email at MacmillanSpecialMarkets@macmillan.com.

Library of Congress Cataloging-in-Publication Data
Names: Cameron, Josephine, author.
Title: Not all heroes / Josephine Cameron.
Description: First edition. | New York: Farrar Straus Giroux Books for Young Readers, 2021. | Audience: Ages 8–12. | Audience: Grades 4–6. | Summary: Moving halfway across the country did not help eleven-year-old Zinnia deal with her little brother's death, but joining her neighbors and aunt as a Real-Life Superhero does that and more.
Identifiers: LCCN 2020039540 | ISBN 9780374314439 (hardcover)
Subjects: CYAC: Crime prevention—Fiction. | Heroes—Fiction. | Aunts—Fiction. | Middle schools—Fiction. | Schools—Fiction. | Moving, Household—Fiction.
Classification: LCC PZ7.1.C327 Her 2021 | DDC [Fic]—dc23
LC record available at https://lccn.loc.gov/2020039540

First edition, 2021
Book design by Cassie Gonzales
Printed in the United States of America by LSC Communications, Harrisonburg, Virginia

ISBN 978-0-374-31443-9 (hardcover)
1   3   5   7   9   10   8   6   4   2

For Mom & Dad, who taught us that love
(and kid power!) can change the world.

And for Uncle Dave, who is even cooler than Papa Wheelie.

Sometimes I worry that no one cares—not about community or compassion, neighbors or lending a helping hand—and I feel a whole ocean of sadness wash over me. But when my team circles up, their kindness is so powerful I can feel that ocean transform. I like to picture it rising, splashing onto rooftops, waterfalling over countries and continents. Can you imagine what it would be like if the entire planet was covered in kindness? *That's* the kind of reality shift I'd like to see.

—Ocean, RLSH

THE HELINSKI FAMILY

Zinnia, age 11

Mom, age 30

Dad, age 34

Aunt Willow, age 19

THE REALITY SHIFTERS ROSTER

Wrecking Ball aka Kris

age: 11

colors: blue and black

skills: orange belt in jiu-jitsu, parkour, reconnaissance

Ocean aka Ekta (formerly known as: Panthalassa, Binary, Sapphire Sting, Chrysalis)

age: 39

colors: ocean blue and black

skills: black belt in jiu-jitsu, culinary arts, emergency medical training

Crystal Warrior aka Emilia

age: 17

colors: pink and red

skills: science, empathic abilities, mental discipline

Silver Sparrow aka Harper

age: 14

colors: black and silver

skills: strength, agility, costume design and gadgetry

Papa Wheelie aka Joe

age: 51

colors: blue and orange

skills: military training, upper arm strength, wisdom of the ages, disability advocacy

Occasional team-ups: Spectrum, Miles, Scar, the eXtreme eXamples

NOT
ALL
HEROES

ONE OCEAN AVENUE

The apartment upstairs goes vacant every few months. Someone gets a new job across town, finds a better place, or gets kicked out. Every time it happens, my parents ask me if we should take it.

"We'd have a better view," Mom says. "I bet you can see all the way to Wing Island from the second floor."

"We'd have a second bathroom," Dad says. "That might be nice."

Nice? It would be heaven. Every morning, Dad gets shaving cream all over the sink. He never notices it, not even when I scrape CLEAN ME! into the scum with my fingernail. And if I leave my toothbrush anywhere in sight, Mom will accidentally use it. Every. Single. Time. Though I've never had a bathroom of my own, I know exactly what it would feel like. It wouldn't feel *nice*. It would feel like freedom.

But even after we all agree that the second-floor apartment is the way to go, no one ever calls the landlord. Instead, we sit in the rocking chairs on the rickety first-floor porch of the two-story house and hash out all the downsides and what-ifs.

We'd have to box everything up again and carry it upstairs. We'd have to rearrange furniture. And what if it didn't pan out? What if the kitchen was too small or we didn't like the color? What if the view wasn't that great, and you couldn't see Wing Island after all?

Which always leads to the same conclusion. We'd already moved halfway across the country. Wasn't that enough? One fresh start was plenty for any family. Especially ours.

We were having this exact conversation the day Kris and Ekta Anand first pulled their tiny green car up to the curb of One Ocean Avenue. Ekta had to duck her head and inch her way out of the driver's seat. It was like a magic trick, watching her long brown limbs unfold out of that jelly-bean car. When she finally stood up to her full height, she stretched, shaded the sun from her eyes, and squinted toward the porch. Almost in unison, all three of our chairs stopped rocking.

"Enjoying the view?" Ekta asked, nodding across the street toward Hilltop Memorial Park and the sparkling bay.

Dad gave an awkward half smile but kept his ocean-blue eyes fixed on the water. Mom wiggled her fingers in the air, then bent down to tie her shoe, her hair conveniently falling forward to hide her face. I squirmed. They could have at least said "Hello."

Kris waved a hand at us from the back seat of the car, and it's hard to remember what I thought of him then. Probably not much beyond "bathroom-stealer." Maybe I would have waved back if their friends hadn't showed up to help them unpack. A minivan arrived first, with a mom, daughter, dad, and son laughing and smiling as they got out of the car. It was impossible to look at that family of four and not think about the person missing from ours. So instead of waving at Kris or shouting out "Welcome to the neighborhood!" I concentrated on picking at the peeling paint on the half-rotted handrail of the porch and waited to see what my parents would do.

I *might* have gotten up and introduced myself when the driver of the minivan—a teenager with giant red glasses, light brown skin, and brown-black curls—waved at me, too. Her smile was so big that the sunlight glinted off her braces. Like the twinkle of a star. Or a flash of lightning. Or maybe that's only how I'm remembering it now. But that was when the girl's mom hopped out of the passenger seat, blond curls bouncing, and started talking a mile a minute about what a great driver her daughter had become and wasn't this the perfect place and couldn't you just *eat up* that view.

Mom and Dad exchanged a look.

Dad stretched, stood up, and turned toward our door.

"I guess that settles that," he said. All nonchalant. Like he'd barely noticed that more people were arriving. A pickup truck piled high with furniture practically drove right up on the front lawn.

Back in Wisconsin, we were the kind of family who would walk down to the cars, ask if we could help, and offer to carry some boxes. We'd make the Anands feel welcome. Lighten their load. But things were different now.

I stood up, too. Mom pushed her hair behind the pink tips of her ears, and we followed Dad inside. It wasn't anything against Ekta or Kris or the friends who'd come to help them move. We weren't trying to be rude. It's just that new people always ask questions that make Mom squirm and Dad pull at his chin until his face slowly morphs from white to flaming red.

It starts out easy-breezy enough. "Where are you from?" and "What brought you to Maine?" Eventually, though, no matter how hard they try to avoid it, conversation always turns to Wally. Smiles disappear. Eyes get droopy. And the frowns turn in my direction. "How's she holding up?" and "Does she miss him?" Like I'm not standing right there.

Of course I miss my brother. But it's not like what people think. Not like what you see in the movies, all dramatic, with some tearful goodbye that I'm always replaying in my mind. It was a regular Sunday. We went to church. Had peanut butter and jelly sandwiches for lunch. It was the last day in September, but we went down to the lake anyway. Made a cold sandcastle. Sat in the canoe and went on one of Wally's "adventures." Except we didn't *actually* go anywhere because he was seven and I was ten and the canoe was tied to the dock. That night, Mom and Wally went to the hospital like they'd done dozens of times. Only this time Wally didn't come home.

Of *course* it's sad. My universe is completely different now that I don't have a little brother constantly asking me to write down stories. But sad doesn't change what happened. Like Dad says, sometimes there's nothing you can do but move on.

We'd thought moving to Maine would make it easier. We'd thought it would be a fresh start away from all the looks and whispers. But it turns out that new people aren't much different from the ones you've known all your life. To new people, it's still a big deal. A big, hairy deal. And they can't move on. So it's better to go inside.

What I didn't realize when I followed Mom and Dad through the front door is that even the smallest action—or *inaction*—has an effect.

It can change the direction of someone else's story.

Or spark a new chapter of your own.

GOODWILL

"Zinnia!"

Mom grabbed at my arm like I was milliseconds away from being roadkill. Even though I was solidly on the sidewalk. Nowhere near the slug-speed traffic that was inching its way through the intersection of Union Street and Chamberlain Avenue.

"You're too close to the curb," Mom said, snugging my arm into hers so she could pull me back to the safe zone.

Walking with my mom in Port City is like being in the middle of a high-stakes video game with fireballs and land mines popping up every few feet. And Mom is In. The. Zone. Three steps ahead of the game, ready to crush every obstacle in her path without using a single turbo-boost or extra life.

"Dog poo!" She jerked me to the left to avoid a steaming pile I wasn't even close to stepping in.

"Eyes straight ahead!" She steered me away from some strangely dressed people crouched in the stairwell of a building.

"Don't even *think* about it. You don't know where that's been." Someone had dropped a set of keys outside Bagel King. I'd barely even glanced at them, but Mom's sixth sense knew I was planning to pick them up.

"What if someone needs them?" I asked.

"What are you going to do? Call up everyone in this city and ask if they lost their keys? Trust me. They've got a spare."

In our old town, she would have let me pick up the keys. There were only a thousand people in Grand Lake, Wisconsin. That town was so small, we probably would have known who the keys belonged to anyway, or at least we could have narrowed it down by the type of car it was. In Port City, there were almost a thousand kids just in my elementary school.

"Okay. It's a big sale, so it's going to be crowded," Mom said as we neared the Goodwill. "You've got your list? And Dad's phone? Set the alarm for one hour and meet me at the checkout. Text me if you want me to come look at anything."

I nodded and followed her into the massive store. Even though it was a zoo, with people everywhere pulling stuff off racks and tables, Mom's shoulders relaxed. As if in here, she knew exactly what to expect, and she didn't have to worry about keeping me safe. She turned toward Housewares and nudged me in the opposite direction toward a bright BACK TO SCHOOL SALE banner.

I unfolded the list Mom had given me and tried to make a plan of action.

winter boots
tennis shoes
jeans
mittens
sweaters
shirts
dress (for Grandma)

I had a twenty-dollar bill from Mom and a twenty from Grandma. It was a rip, but every year, I had to use most of Grandma's birthday money to buy a dress for the first day of school so she could have a photo of me looking "pretty and prepared." She kept a photo album of every first day I'd ever had. She'd started one for Wally, too, but we didn't get to put a lot of pictures in it. Mom says it doesn't matter how much I hate dresses. Sometimes you have to do things you hate for the people you love. Especially grandmas.

I made my way toward a $1.00 SHIRTS table where shoppers were pawing through messy piles of clothes that had probably been neatly folded only an hour ago. There was a line twelve people deep for the changing rooms. This was not going to be a try-it-on situation.

I waited for an opening, then picked through the shirts until I hit the jackpot: a stash of brand-new, plain, long-sleeved T-shirts in multiple colors. I chose seven, one for each day of the week, in every color of the rainbow (I had to substitute aqua for indigo and black for violet, but close enough). I stuffed them into my shopping bag, and checked *shirts* off my list.

I moved on to the jeans and had just maneuvered my way to a decent view of the KIDS' SIZES L–XL table when I spotted a pair of black Doc Martens boots. I picked them up, ran the numbers in my head, and immediately set them down again. The second they hit the table, a girl my age lunged at them. I stepped backward to get out of her way.

"Sorry," I mumbled.

But instead of taking the boots for herself, she pushed them back into my hands.

"What are you *doing*? You *have* to try these on."

"What?"

The girl eyed me. Her hair was tied up into an Afro puff with purple tints hidden in some of her curls. "I've seen you before. Did you go to Oceanside? What size are you?" She didn't take a breath between questions.

I nodded yes to Oceanside Elementary, but I didn't have an answer for the second question. I'd grown an embarrassing two and a half inches since June, and all I knew about my foot size was that my heels were hanging off the backs of my flip-flops.

"Never mind, just try them on. If they fit, you *have* to get them. Good eye, by the way!"

She grabbed my elbow and sat down on the floor, dragging me under the jeans table with her so we'd be out of the way of the frenzied shoppers while I tried on the boots.

"They're twenty dollars," I said, knowing exactly what Mom would say. I could fill my whole bag with one-dollar shirts for the same price as one scuffed-up pair of combat boots.

"I *know*!" the girl said. She loosened the laces on one of the boots and handed it to me with the confidence of a shoe salesperson. "And they're half off. *Ten dollars* for a pair of Doc Martens!"

I removed my sandal and pulled on the boot. It wasn't exactly comfortable—especially in bare feet—but it fit. And it looked *great*. The girl grinned.

"You're so lucky," she said. "I'm still in kids' sizes. It's embarrassing."

I needed winter boots, but these didn't look warm at all. There was no lining or insulation. I wasn't even sure if they were waterproof.

"They're really scuffed up," I said, trying to think of an excuse. I had to put them back.

"That's a good thing! You've got to buy them. It'll kill me if you don't."

I believed her. She seemed like she was in agony, looking at those shoes. I had a harder time believing that she'd recognized *me* out of all the other 999 students at Oceanside Elementary. I'd only gone there for one semester of fifth grade, and I was pretty sure most of the kids in my own classroom didn't know who I was.

"Okay." I knew I wasn't going to leave the store with them, but I put the pair in my shopping bag and checked *winter boots* off my list. It would be easier to put them back after she left.

"I'm Jade." The girl popped a green Jolly Rancher in her mouth and held one out to me.

"No, thanks," I said, even though green Jolly Ranchers are my favorite. I could practically feel the sour apple taste puckering my cheeks. It seemed more polite to say no.

Jade and I crawled out from under the table, and several old ladies scolded us for getting in the way.

"Jade!" A woman with a toddler waved frantically. "I've been looking everywhere! We've got to pick up Bennie!"

Jade said, "See you in school next week, I hope. I'll keep my eye out for those boots!"

I knew it was the kind of thing people say to be nice, but I glanced down at my shopping bag. Maybe I'd hold on to the Docs for a few minutes more.

By the time I got through Mom's list, I was six dollars over budget. Mom found me in the back of the checkout line, sorting through my bag, eyeing the ten-dollar boots and the twelve-dollar dress I'd picked out for Grandma.

Mom picked up the boots and inspected them.

"I know," I said. "They're not practical. I'll put them back."

But she surprised me. "No way. Doc Martens? These are too cool to lose. Here, I found this."

She dug through her overflowing shopping cart and handed me a plain black cotton dress. Five dollars.

"Chuck that other one. You're only going to wear it once."

I grinned. That left me with enough cash to run back and get the pair of rainbow-striped leggings I'd had my eye on. We left the store with our arms full of bags and something close to a warm, hopeful feeling.

As we stepped onto the sidewalk, a red-faced man leaned over in front of Bagel King to pick up the set of keys I'd almost touched. His face lit up like he'd found gold. He was mumbling *Thank the lord* and crossing himself like Catholics do.

"See?" Mom said. "If we'd moved those keys, that guy wouldn't have known where to find them again. Sometimes not helping is really helpful."

"That doesn't make any sense," I said, laughing because we could barely see each other around all the bags we were carrying.

"It's like Grandpa always says. 'You've got enough to take care of in your own backyard.' Don't you think he's right?"

"I guess," I said. But it didn't seem right *not* to help.

On the other hand, the red-faced guy had already jogged a block ahead of us and was happily getting in his car, so maybe she had a point.

14

I was watching him drive away when a young guy in a black sweat suit and a silver helmet smiled and waved at us. The helmet looked old-fashioned, like a gladiator's. It had eyeholes and covered the whole top half of his face, rounding over his nose, and ending in a point shaped like a bird's beak.

The bird-dude said something as we walked past. Not necessarily to us. He said it quietly. Thoughtfully.

"Ka-*kaw*!"

"Eyes straight ahead," Mom said, switching back into video-game mode, and we quickened our pace.

MOOSE ISLAND

School in Port City starts on the Thursday before Labor Day, which is earlier than my old school in Wisconsin. The good news is you only have to go to two days of school before you have a three-day weekend. The bad news is you have to go to school.

As much as I wasn't happy about wearing a dress, at least the one Mom found had pockets, and the rainbow-striped leggings and black Doc Martens took the edge off. I stuffed one of the pockets with green Jolly Ranchers in case I saw Jade, and went into the kitchen to get my photo taken for Grandma's first-day-of-school album.

It felt weird smiling at Mom's camera in the bright blue kitchen of One Ocean Avenue instead of posing at the bus stop with Wally making faces at me. Mom and Dad don't let me ride the school bus in Maine because Mom doesn't trust "random drivers" and Dad doesn't want to lose "quality time." Apparently, whatever official training bus drivers do for their *job* isn't good enough and sitting in traffic listening to the news is a memory-making moment we'll never forget.

Dad was spaced-out during the photo shoot, nibbling at a piece of cinnamon toast and scrolling on his phone. Mom had to nudge him three times to get his attention, and even then, he had a hard time coming back to reality.

"Hm? Yeah, no, right. She looks great." Dad glanced back at his phone a couple of times before he finally set it down and looked at me for real. The expression on his face changed.

"Who's the sixth-grade rock star?" he asked, pretending to look shocked.

"Dad. Stop."

"Seriously. You could be in a punk band dressed like that. You're going to kill it today."

I made a face at him, but I felt decently good for a first day of school. Sixth through eighth graders at Oceanside were in a completely different building across the street from the K–5 kids. Which meant Oceanside Middle School would be about half the size of Oceanside Elementary—five hundred students instead of one thousand.

Even better, all the middle school students got sorted into "islands": Chickadee, Tourmaline, Pine Cone, Moose, and Blueberry. They were named after the Maine state bird, mineral, flower, animal, and berry. Pine cone didn't seem like it should qualify as a flower, but I wasn't going to argue.

The brilliant part was that each island had its own wing of the middle school. So except for assemblies, when everyone had to gather in the gym, you'd feel like there were only about one hundred kids in the whole school. More like Wisconsin. Like home.

I scarfed down my breakfast, peeled the Moose sticker off the Oceanside Middle School welcome packet we'd gotten in the mail, stuck it on my dress, and hefted my backpack onto my shoulders.

"Ready to go?" Dad asked.

"Now or never," I said.

Dad drove me to school and stayed for the Opening Day assembly so he could get some quotes and interview the principal and a few kids. Dad's a reporter for the local public radio station, which isn't as exciting as it sounds. He spends most of his time traveling around the state interviewing the oldest lady in Maine or the family who found a pregnant porcupine living in their shed. Dad's in charge of gathering human-interest stories for the station, but he used to dream about being an announcer, reporting on important world events.

"What are *you* looking forward to learning this year?" he asked in his announcer voice, tipping his recorder in my direction.

"*Dad*," I whispered. I didn't want to be on the radio.

Thankfully, the principal waved at him from her podium, signaling that she was ready for her interview.

"Have a good day, Zinnia. Good luck on the island," he said.

I gave Dad a hug and tried not to feel deserted as he pushed his way through the sea of middle schoolers. Everyone was clustered into groups, hugging and laughing. I recognized a couple kids from fifth grade, but no one I'd ever really talked to. The person I was keeping my eye out for was Jade. I was sure she wouldn't recognize *me*, but I hoped she'd remember my boots. Not that you could see anyone's feet in this packed room. I was glad when the teachers started to sort us into islands. It would be good to get out of this gym.

Someone jostled my backpack and I dropped the paper with my locker combination. When I stood up, Trevor Pryor—with a Moose sticker stuck to his forehead—was sniffing at me.

"Do I smell . . . *chicken?*"

Trevor cracked himself up. I tried to ignore him. Trevor had been part of my "desk pod" at Oceanside Elementary. He'd gotten a haircut over the summer—his usual shaggy blond hair was combed neatly to the side—but otherwise, he hadn't changed one bit.

"Mr. Pryor, can you please put that sticker in a more appropriate place?" A teacher with *Mr. Iftin* on his name tag nodded his chin in our direction.

Trevor snickered and moved the sticker from his forehead to the back pocket of his pants.

The teacher raised his hand and made it clear he was speaking to everyone in our corner of the gym, not just Trevor. "Let's set ourselves up for success this year, okay? I'm so excited about everything we're going to learn, aren't you?"

Trevor caught me looking at him. He peeled the Moose off his butt and put it on the pocket of his polo shirt.

"*I think you have a feather in your hair,*" he whispered. I dodged out of the way as he reached toward my head, grinning, pretending to pick something out of my ponytail. "Don't worry, Chicken! I won't tell anybody."

I gave him a weak smile and moved closer to Mr. Iftin.

Back in January, on my first day at Oceanside Elementary,

I'd spilled chicken soup all over myself at lunch. Trevor Pryor had been playing this bizarre chicken game ever since. He thought it was hilarious. It had started with the whole I-smell-chicken routine, but somehow it grew into an elaborate fantasy world where he pretended that I was *actually* a chicken in disguise. He was always pulling "feathers" off my clothes and clucking at me. Once, I found a hard-boiled egg in my desk. Trevor laughed until he literally had tears streaming down his face.

I kept thinking if I ignored him, he'd get tired of it.

"So, Chicken Little, what homeroom are you in?"

I kept my eyes on Mr. Iftin, silently begging him to lead us out of the gym. Just because Trevor was on Moose Island, didn't *have* to mean he was in my classes. I crossed my fingers inside my pocket and made a wish on a green Jolly Rancher.

"Actually, I guess I can't call you Chicken Little anymore. You got really tall. How many inches did you grow?"

I wasn't going to answer him. Or let him know that I'd heard him at all. But on the inside, I smiled. All summer, I'd felt like a leggy giant. If there was a magic pill that made you stop growing, I would have taken it in an instant. But Trevor hadn't grown a quarter of an inch. Towering over him *was* a little satisfying.

Finally, Mr. Iftin and the other Moose Island teachers ushered us out into the hall.

Trevor kept pace with me, no matter how much I sped up my strides.

"Who do you have for homeroom?" he asked. "I have Iftin."

I uncrossed my fingers. Of course he did.

CHICKEN

It was unbelievable.

In the morning, I had Trevor Pryor in homeroom, Social Studies, study hall, and Math. At lunch, he sat next to me and badgered me with chicken jokes. He must have done some serious research over the summer. I imagined everyone else in his family going to the beach while Trevor stayed home and diabolically plotted out ways to torture me.

"Why did the chicken cross the playground?"

I stuck my fork into the gloppy pile of school-issue mashed potatoes on my tray.

"To get to the other slide. Did you hear the one about the chicken crossing the road?"

I focused on giving no reaction whatsoever. Chew. Swallow. Chew. Swallow.

He didn't get the hint.

"It was poultry in motion."

In Spanish class, Trevor found a new nickname for me: Pollo Loco.

In Science, Ms. Bekker put all our names in a Kleenex box and made us randomly choose a lab partner. Randomly. As in, *You had no idea whose name you were going to pull out.* But guess whose name was on the piece of paper Trevor chose?

"Chicken Nugget . . . I mean, Zinnia Helinski . . . jeez, I almost blew her cover!"

It felt like a conspiracy.

Or dark magic.

There was no possible way we could accidentally have every single class together.

My knees went weak with relief when I walked into Language Arts. It was my final class of the day. My feet were hot. My brain was tired. I needed school to be done. Maybe forever.

But the second I walked in the door, I saw Jade. And as soon as she saw *me*, she waved and smiled.

I looked down at my boots, stuck my hand in my pocket, and gripped a green Jolly Rancher. Jade remembered me. Sixth grade might work out okay after all.

When I raised my hand to wave back, Jade gave a little

squeal. Jumped up from her seat. Waved again. Like she'd forgotten she'd done that already. What a goof.

"I saved you a spot!" she said, still waving.

I grinned and took a step toward the empty desk next to hers when someone—I didn't have to wonder who— bumped into my arm, making me drop the Jolly Rancher. I knew it *had* to be Trevor. I turned around to glare at him.

Instead, a short girl with glasses and two long black braids said, "Sorry!" Then she squealed and ran full speed at Jade.

"Anji!" Jade threw her arms around the girl and sat down beside her. "I can't believe this is the only class we have together! It's not fair! Hey, save that other desk next to you, okay?"

I glued my eyes to my boots again, sat down in the first empty seat I could find, and tried not to think about the long list of things that were not "fair" about this day. Of *course* Jade wasn't waving at me. No one looks that happy to see some random girl they met at Goodwill. My only consolation was that by the time Trevor got to class, the only open seat was all the way in the back of the room. I wished it was even farther. Like Mars.

The kid in the desk next to me bent down and picked up the Jolly Rancher I'd dropped.

"Hey, Zinnia," he said. It was Kris Anand, Ekta's kid. It

was the first thing he'd said to me in the whole two weeks they'd been living upstairs. I wasn't even sure how he knew my name. "Can I have this?"

"Sure."

I put my forehead on my desk. I needed to close my eyes. For thirty seconds. Three minutes, tops. Or maybe just the rest of sixth grade.

We had chicken for dinner. No joke.

I ate the noodles and the broccoli and tried to push the pieces of meat around on my plate so it looked like I'd taken a few bites. Dad didn't even notice. He was all bummed out because the station decided to air an afternoon live panel about a recent crime spike in Port City, so his back-to-school story got shelved.

"Alice is investigating a series of robberies. Dawood's interviewing the new police chief about an increase in teenage vandalism," Dad said. "And *I* reported on the hard-hitting news that your principal's planning to reduce the amount of sugar in the lunchroom by twenty-five percent. Over the next five years."

He put his head in his hands and groaned.

"Why don't you ask to switch departments?" I asked. It

wasn't a new topic. Human-interest stories weren't exactly Dad's passion. Sometimes he got so depressed about his job, he would zone out for hours, scrolling on his phone and forgetting to eat unless Mom and I put food in front of him. Mostly, he'd be thumbing through old photos of us in Wisconsin, but if you asked him what he was thinking about, he'd always say, "Work."

"I can't just ask to switch," he said. "I have to wait for the right time."

"You always say that," I said, and he went back to talking about the school-lunch story that wasn't.

Mom was at the Powerhouse Café until nine because one of the other baristas called in sick at the last second. Someone was always flaking out over there and the owner, Fatuma, called Mom every time. Mom claims it's because she lives the closest, but Dad says it's because she's the only reliable employee Fatuma can trust. I think it's because she makes the best latte art.

Sometimes, when Mom has the evening shift, I walk down to help her close, and she splits her tips with me for sweeping up and cleaning the bathrooms. But after the first day of sixth grade, I barely had the strength to clear my plate.

"How'd it go on the island?" Dad asked, finally taking

a breath from his rant. "Your principal told me about the *Oceanside Sentinel* project the sixth graders are working on. That's pretty cool, right?"

"Uh-huh." I suddenly found the energy to leave the table and start the dishes.

"What'd you sign up for? Editorial? Writing staff? Photography? I mean, writing's more your thing. It's funny, when I was your age, we had a school newspaper, but it was . . . you know, actual *paper*." Dad brought his dishes to the sink. "So?"

"It's not really a newspaper, it's like a . . . literary-journal-website-bloggy thing," I said. "And it's optional."

I hadn't signed up.

"You should do it. You love writing stories. It'd be fun to meet some kids who like the same things you do . . ."

"Mmm." I turned on the garbage disposal to drown out his voice.

I *used* to write stories, but that was only because Wally asked me to, and it was a long time ago. Other than school assignments, I hadn't written anything for a year. Certainly not since we moved to Port City. Yet not a single person in my family had noticed. They acted like it was something I still did all the time. Even Aunt Willow kept sending me blank books.

I had a stack of them sitting on my bedside table.

All empty.

"Well, whatever you want to do," Dad said, trying to act like he wasn't disappointed, even though he obviously was. He got out a dishcloth and started wiping the kitchen counter. "So. Change of subject. Clearly, it wasn't a great day for either of us, but I've got some news that is guaranteed to cheer you up."

I doubted it.

"Aunt Willow's coming for your birthday. Do you mind sharing your bedroom?"

I stopped washing dishes and studied Dad's face. First of all, of *course* I didn't mind. Aunt Willow could use my toothbrush and have all my dessert for a week straight if it meant she was actually coming to see us. Willow is Mom's sister, but she's only eight years older than me and she's the most fun, interesting person in our whole family.

But I needed a little more confirmation before I started celebrating. Willow started college last year, and ever since, she's been too busy writing some paper or rehearsing with her band to call or visit. She plays guitar in a "jazz-rock fusion cooperative" and personally, I think the music sounds horrible, but Dad says they're objectively great, so what do I know? The point is, it wouldn't be the first time

Aunt Willow promised to come and then changed her mind at the last minute.

"Didn't she get that research scholarship, though?" I asked. "Mom said that was a big deal. It's like a job, right? She probably can't leave if she needs to help the professor."

I tried to keep my breath steady and even. Like I *should* have done before waving like a dope at Jade in Language Arts class. The trick is to expect the worst. Then you can't be disappointed.

"Zinnia." Dad smiled and put his hand on my shoulder. He shook it a little, trying to loosen me up. "You can relax. She'll show up this time. She has a plane ticket and everything."

SPANDEX

I spent the weekend cleaning my room and setting up my sleeping bag on the floor, even though Willow wasn't coming for two weeks. I wanted to be ready. Plus, I have a love-hate relationship with straightening up, so I figured I might as well do it while I felt motivated.

The hate part is obvious. Who likes cleaning?

The love part is that I always find something I'd forgotten about. Like Mom's binoculars hidden under a towel near my closet door.

I took the binoculars to my bed and leaned against the window. There's not a lot to see in our backyard. The house is shaped like an L, and my bedroom's in the back. Which means I can't see the ocean or the park or even the street because the front of the house blocks my view of everything but a giant oak tree, the bird feeder only I remember to fill, and the second-floor apartment window. The Anands had taken down the lacy curtains from the last tenant and put up dark green blinds. That's about the extent of the excitement that happens from my view.

I focused in on three goldfinches fighting over the bird feeder. The right binocular lens was all messed up and blurry, and it took me awhile to adjust it until I could see the yellow and black feathers clearly. Two of the birds had settled into an agreement to share the feeder and ice the third bird out, and I'd just zeroed in on them when a scraping sound from upstairs sent them darting off into the oak tree.

I turned my binoculars toward the second floor.

Kris Anand had pulled up the green blinds and removed the window screen. The top of his head was in perfect focus in my lenses. I could almost see every strand of black hair bouncing while he bent over the sill, examining something below. I set down the binoculars and scooted back so my rainbow-striped curtain would cover me.

From behind my curtain, I could see he was messing with an ancient metal fire escape below the window. With a terrible high-pitched screech, the ladder creaked, released, and dropped toward the ground. Kris straightened up, and I grabbed my binoculars again.

He had a black mask tied over his eyes. Like the kind the Incredibles wear.

He stretched a leg over the windowsill. Revealing blue spandex tights.

Kris put his foot on the first rung, tested the ladder for sturdiness, then shimmied down to the ground. In a full-on blue bodysuit with a black Speedo over the leggings.

I would have thought he was sneaking out, except that Ekta showed up right behind him. Her long legs—also covered in blue spandex—snaked out the window and down the fire escape. As soon as her feet hit the ground, she high-fived Kris, and he climbed back up the ladder and wriggled back in through the second-floor window. They did this twice before our phone started ringing. Down. Up. Down. Up. High-fiving and taking turns climbing in and out of the house.

I waited a couple rings for Dad to answer the phone, but he hates distractions when he's working on a deadline, so eventually, I had to tear myself away from the window.

"Hey ZZ, it's Aunt Willow. What's going on?"

"Oh, uh . . . hey, Willow."

Normally, one of Aunt Willow's rare phone calls would make me drop everything to ask her all the news. But the stuff that was happening in my backyard wasn't exactly normal.

"Everything okay, Z?" Aunt Willow asked.

"Yeah. Fine," I said, trying to keep my voice down while I carried the phone to my bedroom and went back to my station at the window. Ekta and Kris were still at it. Climbing up and down the fire escape. At one point, Kris took a running leap at the oak tree, ran three or four steps *up* the tree, then flipped down and headed back to the fire escape. Like gravity didn't apply.

I barely breathed behind my rainbow curtain.

"Zinnia?" Willow sounded concerned. "Are you still there? What's wrong?"

"Nothing. Just. Our new neighbors are . . . a little different."

Ever since the Anands moved in, I'd been hearing strange noises upstairs. Thumps. Crashes. Mom said they must be moving furniture, but Dad thought it sounded more like they had a small elephant for a pet.

"Hear that?" he'd say. "They're playing fetch with Dumbo."

Now, Ekta, in her blue-and-black spandex, followed Kris up the fire escape one last time.

Hoisted herself into the upstairs apartment.

Closed the window.

Lowered the blinds.

I waited, but they seemed to be done with . . . whatever that was.

"Earth to ZZ," Willow said in a singsong voice. "Your dad told me you didn't sign up for the class journal. What's up with that? You love writing. Are you working on any new adventure stories?"

I leaned back into my pillow and eyed the stack of empty blank books Aunt Willow had sent me. It was bad enough disappointing Dad. Letting Willow down was almost unbearable.

"I don't know. I'm just not . . ."

I paused long enough that Willow had to fill in the blanks.

"As into it as you used to be?"

"Right," I said.

"I get it."

I relaxed into my pillow. Willow didn't sound disappointed. She sounded like she understood.

"Parents can be so weird that way," she said. "It's like they expect you to stay six years old your whole life. My dad still sends me Play-Doh in my care packages."

"He does not!" I cracked up and Willow laughed, too.

"Not really," she said. "But practically. He really does treat me like a baby sometimes. Hey, did you hear I'm coming for your birthday?"

"Yes!" I said. "But how? Don't you have school?"

Now it was Willow's turn to be quiet. I checked the second-floor window, but nothing was happening. The goldfinches had come back to the feeder and one of them dive-bombed the others, trying to scare them off.

"I don't know, Z," she said finally. "Maybe I'm not as into that anymore, either, you know?"

"What do you mean? I thought you loved college."

"I do. I mean, I did. But . . . I spent all last year reciting Shakespeare and learning how to mimic Miles Davis solos on the guitar."

"That sounds cool."

"Sure, but it's not *useful*. To the world, you know? What's the point? What am I doing with my life? I'm just sort of . . . stuck."

I lay all the way down on my bed and stared at the ceiling. In the daylight, my glow-in-the-dark stars looked dirty and yellow. I'd put them up when we first moved to Port City to remind me of home. When Aunt Willow was still in high school, she used to come for sleepovers and we'd bring sleeping bags out to the dock and watch the stars. Wally and I would cozy up, one on each side, and Willow would tell us stories about the constellations. Adventure stories. Wally's favorite kind. I always asked for the one about Cygnus the Swan, even though it's sad and in the end, Cygnus loses his best friend and never finds him again. I hated that part, but I loved that Cygnus never gives up looking.

"Sometimes I feel really lost, Z," Aunt Willow said. Her voice was soft. Lonely.

Me too, I thought, trying not to notice my empty sleeping bag on the floor.

"It's a good thing you're coming to Maine."

AUNT WILLOW

When we picked Willow up from the airport, she had her guitar, a small travel-sized amplifier, a metal-framed back-pack almost as tall as me, and two suitcases.

"That's a lot of stuff for a long weekend," Dad said. He grunted as he hoisted the backpack onto his shoulder. "What's in here, bricks?"

Willow shrugged. "I thought I'd do some laundry."

"You know they have washing machines in Wisconsin, right?" Dad teased. "I would have sent you the quarters for the Laundromat. What's up with the amp? Are you playing a gig?"

"I thought ZZ and I might want to jam."

I grinned. I couldn't play anything, but I loved listening to Willow practice.

"I'll get it," I said. I picked up the amp by the leather han-dle. "I can carry the guitar, too."

Willow's guitar was always heavier than I thought it was going to be. The beat-up case was made out of wood, and if you carried it too long, it made your arm feel like it was going to fall out of its socket. But I felt good lugging it around. Important. Proud. Like Aunt Willow was a rock star and I was her roadie.

It was a Friday night, so after we dropped Willow's luggage in my bedroom, the three of us walked down the street to visit Mom at the café. When the cheery lights of the Powerhouse came into sight, my shoulders suddenly tightened and my feet stopped moving. It was too weird. How were we supposed to *be*? The four of us, all together again, without Wally? And how was Mom going to feel? My cheeks got hot, and I felt Dad's arm around my shoulders.

"Fresh start," he whispered. Like he could read my mind. Or maybe he was feeling the same thing. He tugged me forward until I started walking again, and then he put on a cheerful voice. "Wait'll you see her face," he said. "I think Mom's missed Willow even more than you have."

He wasn't wrong. Mom's grin when she saw her little sister made my spine go all tingly. I hadn't realized how long it had been since I'd seen her look *happy* like that. Even though the café was packed and there was a line of customers, she took the time to make us all special drinks that weren't on the menu—honey hot chocolate for me, orange-flavored mocha for Dad, and a cinnamon latte topped with whipped cream and caramel for Willow.

When the last customer finally left, we helped Mom empty all the coffee pots and clean the tables, and then we went next door for late-night pizza and root beer. The strange thing was that it didn't feel strange at all. It felt great. Mom, Dad, and Willow told hilarious old stories and we laughed until they took my root beer away because I kept spitting it up. Something inside of me started to relax. Maybe this was what a fresh start felt like. Maybe *this* was how Maine was supposed to feel all along. We'd just been missing something.

We splurged on a brownie sundae to share, and while Dad and I shoveled globs of hot fudge lava into our mouths, Mom's mood shifted. She got all teary-eyed, but not in the way I'd expected. Her wet eyes weren't about Wally or even about why Willow never visited or called. Mom shook her head at her sister in a schmoopy kind of way.

"What?" Willow squirmed.

"Look at you. You're nineteen. You're a *research fellow*."

I gave Willow a chocolaty grin, and she blushed.

"It's not that big of a deal," she said.

"When *I* was nineteen, all I was doing was changing Zinnia's poopy diapers," Mom said.

"Mom! Gross!"

Aunt Willow threw an arm around me and pulled me close until I almost fell off my chair.

"Best thing you ever did," she said. "ZZ is worth twenty scholarships. At least."

Then she picked the last three cherries off the brownie sundae and put them on my plate so no one could eat them but me.

When we finally went to bed, it was eleven o'clock, but Aunt Willow and I stayed up talking for another half hour— Willow in my bed, and me in my sleeping bag on the floor. She asked me what I'd been reading and what I liked to do in Maine. I told her about my favorite spot in the park across the street from our apartment. I even told her about Trevor and Jade. Sort of. I told her there was a boy who made chicken jokes about me. And that Jade had finally noticed me in the hallway, and said, "Nice boots!" and I didn't say anything back. My voice had stuck in my throat and I'd stared at the scuffed-up tips of my boots until she walked away.

"Can I tell you a secret, Z?" Aunt Willow whispered.

"Yeah. Of course."

"I don't think I'm going to go back to college."

"Really?" I thought of all the stuff she'd brought with her and I felt my heart flutter.

"Are you going to stay here?" I asked.

"Maybe. It depends."

"On . . . ?"

"I don't know. I need to find *something*. Something that matters," she said. "An adventure. A purpose. I don't want to sleepwalk through life. Do you?"

"No," I said. Part of me knew I shouldn't get my hopes up, but I let myself do it anyway. I breathed into my sleeping bag and imagined how different life would be with Aunt Willow around. For some reason, Kris and Ekta's moving day popped into my brain. All their friends smiling and helping. Showing up.

That, I thought. *It would feel like* that.

"I want to make a pact, ZZ. Let's help each other be adventurous, okay? No more sleepwalking. No more letting life pass us by."

The flutter in my heart sped up. "Okay," I said. "It's a pact." It felt like an important moment. The kind of moment that always happens in a book or a movie before the world is turned upside down and everything changes irreversibly.

A loud bang from the upstairs apartment made me flinch, and Willow let out a small yelp of surprise. The elephant noises began. *Thump. Pound. Crash.*

"What *is* that?" Willow turned on the bedside lamp, eyes wide.

"I have no idea," I said. "It happens all the time. Especially on the weekends."

"It sounds like they're jump-roping," Willow said, and the thought of Kris and Ekta playing double Dutch in the middle of the night made me start to giggle. Willow giggled, too, as we listened to the Anands playing hopscotch or basketball or whatever it was they were doing up there.

"Okay. Second pact," Willow said. "We are going to find out what *that's* all about."

She didn't know the half of it. I was about to tell Aunt Willow about the fire escape and the blue bodysuits, but before I could stop laughing, Mom knocked on the door.

"Settle down in there!" Her voice sounded stern from the hall. "Lights out!"

"Oh my gosh, Jen, you sound like Mom!" Willow threw her pillow at the door and it slid to the floor with a soft *thump*. "It's not even a school night."

The door opened and Mom stuck her head in. She was grinning. Holding her own pillow and blankets.

"Scoot over, Zinnia," she said, tossing her stuff on the floor next to me. "You guys are having all the fun. It's not fair."

I spread Mom's blankets next to my sleeping bag while she jumped on my bed and pummeled Willow with the pillow my aunt had thrown.

"Remember how you used to sabotage my high school

sleepovers with Marty and Meeghan? I still haven't paid you back for that."

"Sabotage?" Willow held her arms up against the attack. "My pillow-bombs made them *better*! Admit it. Marty and Meeghan liked me better than you."

"You were in kindergarten!"

"I was very mature for my age."

I'm pretty sure I fell asleep smiling, listening to Mom and Willow chatting, and the neighbors playing fetch with Dumbo upstairs. But I woke up worrying. About adventures and how to find them.

I'd promised Aunt Willow I'd help her find that *something* she was looking for, but Wally had been the expert on adventures, not me. I was only the historian who wrote them down.

"It's easy, Zin," he would say, probably after sticking his stinky feet in my face or burping his apple juice breath in my direction. "Adventures are everywhere."

I hoped he was right. Because after Willow's first night in Maine—after all the laughing and hugs and extra cherries—I already knew I couldn't go back to a three-person life. In Wisconsin, we'd had friends. Family. Wally. Here, it was just me, Mom, and Dad alone in the world.

Until Aunt Willow arrived, I hadn't realized how much I needed more.

HILLTOP MEMORIAL PARK

The next morning was a Saturday, and Mom and Dad were gone before Willow woke up. Mom had the opening shift at the café, and Dad had to drive two hours north to interview some farmers about their heirloom apple orchard.

I made Willow waffles with Maine blueberries and Maine maple syrup, then put her coffee into a to-go cup and took her across the street to show off Hilltop Memorial Park. Nothing adventurous ever happened there, but it was my favorite spot in Port City. There was a walking trail lined with benches that wound down the hill—past a playground, a World War II memorial with a hundred soldiers' names chiseled into concrete slabs, and all the way to a pebbled, leash-free beach where people brought their dogs to play Frisbee and splash around in Memorial Bay. It wasn't enough to keep Willow in Maine, but I hoped it was a start.

I led her over an outcropping of rocks where we found dozens of snails and two hermit crabs hanging out in the tide pools. I showed her how if you hold a periwinkle in the palm of your hand and hum to it, the snail comes out of its shell and dances around. Willow made me hold her coffee while she picked up snail after snail, humming until their slimy antennae poked out and waved in the air.

"How did I not know about this?" she asked, grinning.

"You've never visited Maine before."

"Fair."

Behind the pebble beach was an abandoned railroad track. We crossed over it and picked up the walking path again, following it back up the hill toward the playground. The hill is steeper than it seems and we were both out of breath by the time we got to the top. I paused at a park bench under a big maple tree, directly across the street from One Ocean Avenue.

"Here it is," I said, sitting down on the bench, breathing hard. "My spot."

Willow laughed, but she was so winded from the hill, it came out more like a wheeze. "Seriously? This is exactly where we started. I could throw a rock and hit your house!"

"I know," I said. "I like it because it's the only bench on the whole path that's shady. And you can see everything."

I pointed to all the places we'd just been. The playground. The memorial. The beach. The tide pools. The railroad tracks. From my bench, you could see all of that, plus the entire bay dotted with boats and buoys.

Willow's eyes rested on a small bronze plaque on the backrest of the bench, but I shook my head and looked out at the bay.

"All the benches in Memorial Park have something like that," I said. "You just . . . rest your back on it."

Willow sat down next to me and leaned against the plaque.

"It looks like Grand Lake," she said.

It did, a little. Most of the bay was lined with trees, and there were never any waves. The only hints that you weren't looking at a lake were the lobster buoys and a small patch of water that wasn't bound in by trees. If you took a boat to that edge of Memorial Bay and kept going, you'd be all the way out in the Atlantic Ocean, surrounded by nothing but water for miles.

"It's a good spot," Willow said. "What do you do here?"

"Watch people." I cringed at how boring that sounded and added more. "That lady's been training her dog but it's not working." I pointed to an elderly woman down at the beach who was making hand motions toward a black pug who was much more interested in the seagulls. "And that guy loves the swings." In the playground, there were several kids playing on the slides and the monkey bars, but a man was on the swing set, pumping his legs and singing at the top of his lungs while a lady in a uniform read a book on a nearby bench. "I think that woman's his aide. Or his mom. I've seen them outside the group home on Union Street. They're here almost every day."

Willow smiled. "He seems really happy."

"I think he'd swing all day if she let him."

"There's an interesting character." Willow nudged my arm and waved her coffee cup in the direction of someone jogging up the hill from the railroad track.

"I've seen him before," I said, and even though I couldn't possibly have *known* anything that was going to happen next, I leaned forward on the bench to get a better look. Like watching some guy jog up a hill was the most life-changing part of my day. I mean. Maybe it was.

The guy was large, like a high school football player, with legs and arms the size of small tree trunks, and his belly bounced a little each time his silver sneakers hit the ground. He was breathing hard, but not gasping for air like Willow and I had been, and we'd only been walking. He wore a black sweat suit with a wide silver waistband and he held a pair of weights in his hands—in case running up a massively steep incline wasn't enough exercise.

"Can you imagine *jogging* up that hill?" Willow asked. "I'd be dead."

The jogging looked tough, but the thing I couldn't look away from was the silver gladiator helmet that curved over his head, forming a point around his nose like a bird's beak. It was hard to see his eyes through the eyeholes, but he clearly caught me staring because he smiled and lifted his brown chin at us as he passed our bench, then hooked a left toward the road behind us.

The second he took the turn, a voice rang out from somewhere above our heads.

"Come on, Silver Sparrow! You've got this! PUSH IT!!!!"

Aunt Willow and I swiveled on the bench and watched as the guy sprinted across the street.

Up the sidewalk.

And straight through the front door of One Ocean Avenue.

REAL-LIFE SUPERHEROES

"I don't want to knock. *You* knock," I whispered.

"This was our pact, Z." Aunt Willow grinned and nodded toward the door of the Anands' upstairs apartment. "I'm helping you be more adventurous."

I swallowed a groan. Regret had hit me pretty hard about halfway up the stairs. I didn't actually want to *be* more adventurous. But I did want Willow to stay. The way she was grinning—the way she hadn't *stopped* grinning since Silver Sparrow ran past us in the park—I didn't really have a choice. I tightened my grip on our "welcome gift" of coffee beans we'd stolen from Mom's stash and raised my other fist.

The door swung open before my knuckles had a chance to hit the wood.

"I told you there was a noise in the hall," Ekta said to

someone inside the apartment. She didn't smile at us or say hello. She stood, a good six inches taller than Willow, and stared us down. It was more nerve-racking than you'd think because her black hair was pulled back into a severe pony-tail, and she was dressed in the blue spandex bodysuit and black Speedo I'd seen her wear on the fire escape. Her eyes blinked behind a black fabric mask like a superhero straight out of a comic book. Looking at her in that moment, it wasn't too far a stretch to think Kris's mom might be able to hurl a lightning bolt at the wall.

Willow nudged my elbow. Still grinning.

"I'm Zinnia and this is my aunt, Willow," I said. "We wanted to introduce ourselves. Welcome you to the neighborhood."

"Oh really, now?" Ekta said. She pressed her lips into a tight, skeptical smile. I squirmed.

Over her shoulder, I could see the guy in the silver helmet doing push-ups in the living room while some-one counted excitedly. "Twenty-two . . . twenty-three . . . twenty-four . . ."

Willow took the bag of coffee beans from my useless hand and held it out.

"We brought you coffee," she said. "It's Powerhouse. The good stuff."

"Twenty-five!" the person inside shouted, and suddenly,

Kris and Silver Sparrow were at the door. Kris was dressed in blue-and-black spandex, like his mom. Up close, I could see the outline of his black mask was cut in a jagged pattern that made it look more dramatic than it had seemed through binoculars.

"Sparrow's done. We're ready to go," he said. "Oh, hey, Zinnia."

The guy in the helmet took a swig from a squeeze bottle, then smiled a sweaty smile. "I've seen you two." He sounded a *lot* younger than he looked. Maybe he wasn't a high school football player after all, but he was definitely training like one.

A teenager appeared at the now-crowded doorway, waving her phone. She wasn't wearing a mask, but behind her glasses she had elaborate, sparkly face paint around her eyes. She wore red leggings and a flowing red top cinched around the waist with a wide utility belt that reminded me of the kind Batman wears—only hers was pink.

"Everything's ready at the pickup spot," she said. "Oh. *You.*"

The girl had been smiling when she came to the door, but the smile disappeared when she saw me. Even in the costume, I recognized her. She was the teenager who'd been driving the minivan the day Kris and Ekta moved in.

The minivan with the family of four. She adjusted her red glasses and ran her tongue over her braces before giving me the sad, I'm-so-sorry-for-your-loss look that people usually give after they hear about Wally. But this girl didn't know anything about my brother.

"Are you guys cosplayers?" Willow asked. "Is there a comic convention today?"

Ekta rolled her eyes. "I'll get the stuff," she said to the others. "Ready to roll in three minutes, okay? Thanks for the coffee beans . . . *neighbors.*" She gave a sarcastic salute before disappearing into the apartment.

The girl with the braces still had me in an eye lock. She wore a choker around her neck that was making me uncomfortable. Embedded in the center of the choker was a pink stone with spidery white lines that formed a star. Only what it really looked like was an eye. And it was staring straight at me. I stepped closer to Willow, and I am not kidding, the eye followed.

The teenager caught me looking at the stone and she tapped it with her fingers.

"It's a crystal," she said. "Pink star sapphire. It's tuned to the heart. So. Can I ask you a question about yours?"

My heart? She wanted to ask me a question about my *heart?* I didn't know what else to do. I nodded.

"Why now?" the girl asked.

Why what? I looked at Willow. She shrugged.

"You couldn't even say hello?" The girl looked so disappointed I wanted to melt into a puddle and disappear down the stairs.

"What's she talking about?" Willow whispered in my ear.

I wasn't exactly sure, but I had a guess. "I . . . when they moved in . . . we—"

"Completely ignored us?" Ekta called from the kitchen. "Treated us like we were invisible for a whole month now?"

I felt miserable. Even Willow looked embarrassed. I didn't know how to explain that my parents never talked to *anyone* new unless they had to for work. Not that it mattered. She wasn't asking about my parents, she was looking at *me*.

"I'm really sorry," I mumbled. "We didn't mean to make you feel bad."

"Zinnia's all right," Kris said to the girl. Even behind his mask, I could tell he felt sorry for me. "She gave me a Jolly Rancher at school. We're good."

The girl put her hand on the pink star-eye at her neck and seemed to think for a minute. Then she shone her smile straight at me.

"I'm glad you came upstairs today," she said in a tone

that almost *forced* me to believe she meant it. "It's never too late to be kind."

I was so relieved to be let off the hook, and she looked so nice and friendly even in her funny costume, that I had a burst of courage. Not a big one. Just enough to ask the question we'd come for.

"Why are you dressed up like that?" I'd already tried to think of the possibilities. A kid's birthday party. A costume contest. Though neither option explained the fire escape drills Kris and Ekta had been doing in the backyard.

"We're RLSH," she said. "Real-Life Superheroes."

"Wait," Willow said. "Repeat that."

"I'm Crystal Warrior. This is my little brother, Silver Sparrow."

"Ka-kaw!" Silver Sparrow burst out, and then immediately looked embarrassed. "I know that's not what a sparrow sounds like—"

"But it works," Kris jumped in with a reassuring nod. Silver Sparrow towered over both of them. "Little" had to be a joke. Like "superheroes." Willow touched my elbow. I was certain it was a let's-get-out-of-here signal, which was fine with me. Crystal Warrior seemed nice, but we'd been adventurous enough.

Only I was wrong. Willow had no intention of leaving.

"Do you have . . . super*powers*?" she asked.

"No," Kris said.

But Crystal Warrior shushed him and put her hands on her hips in a serious superhero stance.

"We have the power to help the helpless." She made her voice all bold and filled with urgency. Like she was on a movie set and the cameras were zooming in. "We have the power to bring hope to the hopeless. We can give people a voice and speak up when we see injustice. Empathy is a superpower. Caring is a superpower. *Courage* is a *superpower*!"

As uncomfortable as I felt, there was something about the way Crystal Warrior talked that was extra-impressive. I thought about applauding but that would be weird.

"So it's like a heroes club?" I asked instead.

Kris and Silver Sparrow cracked up and Crystal Warrior wrinkled her nose.

"It's not a club, it's a *league*," Kris said. "A *team*."

"Isn't that the same thing?" I asked, and Silver Sparrow hooted.

"We're called the Reality Shifters." Ekta suddenly showed up at the door with an armful of backpacks. "And if it'll satisfy your bottomless curiosity, we're on a mission to assist people who don't have anywhere to sleep tonight, so we don't have time to stand here and yak all day. *If* you all don't mind."

Kris and Silver Sparrow hopped to attention and grabbed two backpacks out of her arms.

"Bye, Zinnia!" Kris said as they followed Ekta down the stairs.

Crystal Warrior stayed where she was and studied us one last time. I got the distinct feeling that she—or her eerie star-eye necklace—was looking into our souls.

"I *see* you," she said, as if to confirm it. "You have powers, too. Please don't waste them."

Crystal Warrior's eyes pinned me, and for a second I felt like I couldn't move. I was on the tips of my toes, breath sucked in. And then Aunt Willow did something I did not see coming.

She opened her mouth and asked, "Can we come with you? On the mission?"

She couldn't be serious. There was no way my parents would be okay with us going anywhere with a bunch of strangers. In costumes. But Willow was lit up. Her eyes were shining. Her grin had practically taken over her whole face.

"This is it," she said. "Right, Zinnia?"

I knew what she was trying to tell me. Willow had found her *something*. Her adventure. Her purpose. So I pretended not to know how mad Mom would be, and I swallowed the fact that I was sort-of-maybe-definitely scared of Ekta. What was harder to ignore was that Crystal Warrior was wrong about me. I didn't have *any* of the powers she was talking about. Courage? The power to bring help to the helpless? I was the farthest thing from a superhero. How was *I* supposed to help?

In the end, I swallowed that, too. Because Aunt Willow reached out and squeezed my hand and I really, *really* didn't want her to let go.

"Right," I said. "We want to come."

REALITY SHIFTERS

"Nope." Ekta tossed the last backpack into the minivan and slammed down the rear door. "We don't have time today. I'm all for new recruits, but . . . I don't think these two have what it takes."

She didn't even bother to lower her voice. I coughed in case she didn't remember we were standing right there.

"No offense." Ekta shrugged at me. "Lots of people *think* they want to be RLSH but it's not glamorous. It's hard work. Frankly, I don't like it when people get into it for the wrong reasons."

"We're not afraid of hard work," Willow said. "We have good reasons."

"*Everyone* deserves a chance to—" Crystal Warrior sounded like she was starting a speech, but Ekta cut her off.

"Fine. Tell me your reason," she said, pointing at me.

I must have looked like I was going to panic and mess everything up because Willow jumped right in. "We want to—"

"Not you. Her." Ekta's masked eyes were on me. "Why do you want to be a superhero?"

I didn't *have* a reason because I didn't want to *be* a superhero and Ekta knew it. Willow looked worried. Like she knew I was going to ruin this for her.

"Wally would have liked it," I blurted, and immediately regretted it. Why did I say *that*?

"Who's Wally?"

"Her brother," Willow said when I didn't answer. "I mean . . . he *was*. He had brain cancer."

I braced myself for the awkward silence, the *I'm so sorrys*, and the sad-eyed shoulder pats that always come next. But all that happened was that Silver Sparrow said, "I've got extra eye masks," and Ekta said, "Don't blame me if you don't like it," and Crystal Warrior got in the driver's seat of the van, and the rest of them piled in after her.

"Come on, Zin," Kris said. "You can sit in the way-back with me and Sparrow."

I stared at him, one foot in and one foot out of the van. Part of my brain noticed that it wasn't your usual minivan.

The back was a typical three-seater, but the whole middle section was wide open, with only a jumpseat on the driver's side that could fold up and out of the way. But most of my brain was focused on Kris's words. *Come on, Zin.*

My brother used to call me Zin. I'd felt a jolt at the sound. For a second, it froze me, but Willow, already in the jumpseat, reached out her warm hand and I let her pull me in.

According to Kris, the minivan belonged to Crystal Warrior and Silver Sparrow's uncle, Papa Wheelie, who was at the "pickup point" right now, setting everything up.

"Crystal dropped Wheelie off before she came to get us," Kris said. "Wait till you see his wheelchair. It's all tricked out."

"Mom gets home at four," I reminded Willow. I was trying to tell her: *We can still back out.*

Aunt Willow didn't seem remotely concerned. She was going through the details of the mission with Ekta and putting location points into her phone. Making plans with superheroes like she did it every day.

Crystal Warrior looked at me in the rearview mirror and gave a thumbs-up. "I told my dad we'd be home before that anyway."

Kris turned toward me. "Try not to use our regular names, okay? Superhero names only when we're on patrol."

I hadn't expected Kris to talk to me. I hadn't expected him to talk at all, he was so quiet at school. Classroom invisibility was apparently a trick we had in common. But he hadn't *stopped* talking since we got in the van.

"My mom is Ocean, though she might want to be called Panthalassa. She's still deciding if that's catchy enough. She used to be Chrysalis. Binary before that. Sometimes you've got to try out a few before you find your true name."

"What's Panthalassa?"

"Did you learn plate tectonics in fourth grade? How all the continents used to be one big landmass?"

I nodded.

"Panthalassa was the name of the one ocean," he said. "Mom thought of it when we moved to the new apartment. *One Ocean* Avenue. You know?"

"What are you called?" I asked.

Kris smirked. "Wrecking Ball."

It was a good name, and he knew it. I started to relax again. Maybe Mom and Dad wouldn't mind if I was hanging out with a kid from my class. They might be glad, actually.

Silver Sparrow had been rummaging through his backpack. "Ka-*kaw*!" he said, and handed me and Willow each a black eye mask and a pair of heavy-duty gloves with sleeves that went up past my elbows.

"I always have spares," he said. "You can give them back after you make your own gimmick."

"What's a gimmick?" I laid the gloves and the eye mask in my lap instead of putting them on. I felt silly wearing a costume in the middle of the day when it wasn't Halloween.

"It's like your persona," Kris said. "Your outfit, tool kit, your name. Sparrow does most of our design and gadgetry 'cause he's a genius at it. He *made* that helmet."

"Seriously?" It looked like something passed down from the Middle Ages.

Silver Sparrow grinned. "You can't tell, but it's mostly masking tape and spray paint," he said. "I've got a lot of practice. If you need help making yours."

Making *mine*? Like I was ever going to do this again?

I looked at Willow in the small middle seat. She pulled her gloves up over her sweatshirt sleeves and turned to give me a high five. She didn't look anything like a super-hero. A masked bandit, maybe.

"Put yours on," she said. "You'll look great!"

I pulled the mask over my eyes and took a breath. It was strange how something as simple as a mask could change your whole view. Looking through the eyeholes, my periph-eral vision was blocked, and I could only see what was right in front of me. The world felt smaller, but somehow, *I* felt bigger. Like with all that extra black space surrounding me, I had less to worry about. Room to breathe.

"Ready for adventure!" Willow said, and turned back to chat with Ekta and Crystal Warrior.

"It's good you're here," Kris said. "Papa Wheelie couldn't convince any of the eXamples to come."

"The what?"

He checked the front seat to make sure Ekta wasn't paying attention before launching into the history of the Port City Real-Life Superheroes. Apparently, Kris's group used to be part of another RLSH league called the eXtreme eXamples. But they were in some kind of frenemy situation and now the Reality Shifters were doing their own thing.

"There are *two* superhero clubs in Port City?" I asked. "How come you're not all over the news?" This definitely seemed like the kind of thing Dad's station would ask him to report.

"*Leagues*," Kris said. "And I don't know, people don't notice us like that. The eXtreme eXamples only do night patrol, and they're stealthy about it. Even on day patrol, people usually think we're out for photo ops or going to a comic-book thing."

"Or they think we're weirdos," Sparrow added.

"Either way," Kris said. "We're kind of invisible. Even when people see us."

That made sense. Mom and I had seen Silver Sparrow in broad daylight outside Goodwill and the last thing I thought was "superhero."

"Anyway, day patrol is usually humanitarian stuff like this blanket mission. Night patrol's for crime-fighting. It's a lot more intense, but I've got an orange belt in jiu-jitsu, so it's safe. Mom's a black belt. She's fierce."

I stared at Kris. "You fight crime?"

"I mean, I'm still in training, so I don't do a lot of night patrol."

Silver Sparrow had taken a container of cold spaghetti noodles out of his bag and was scarfing them down. He paused to cough and poke his beak toward Kris.

"Okay, we're not allowed on night patrol until we're eighteen. But yeah." Kris gave me side-eye. Like it was the most obvious thing on the planet, and I was the weirdo for even asking. "We're superheroes. Of course we fight crime."

Silver Sparrow picked up a noodle and whipped it at Kris.

"Fine, I haven't seen a crime yet," Kris said. "But I would fight it if I did."

Sparrow shook his head.

"What?" Kris blurted. "Of course we would! Zinnia would, too."

"I would?" I doubted it.

"My dad's stressed out enough about day patrol."
Sparrow was still shaking his head. "I have to hear the
safety talk three times a week. At least."

My eyes got wide. Safety talk? "Is day patrol . . . dangerous?" I asked.

"No," Kris said. "We're helping people."

But Sparrow shrugged. "Dad says wearing masks makes
it easy for people to mistake us for bad guys. Probably not
you, Zinnia. But me. Or Kris."

"But we're *helping* people," Kris repeated.

"You've heard him," Sparrow said. "*Son, always be extra-
polite out there and never put your hands in your pockets and
never, ever talk back to the police*," he mimicked, putting
on a funny, deep Dad voice that made me think Sparrow's
dad and my mom could play protective-parent video games
together.

Then he got serious. "I mean. He's right. Brown kids have
to be more careful. Especially boys. But I'll probably still do
night patrol. When I'm old enough."

Kris sighed at the word *probably*, and I sighed, too.
Because it wasn't fair that Kris and Sparrow should have
to be more careful than me just because of how they
looked.

"Your dad still lets you do day patrols, though?" I asked.

"Yeah, he gets it. Like Kris said, we're helping people.

And he thinks that my goofy bird helmet is less threatening than a regular mask."

"Really?" I looked at Kris in his jagged black eye mask and then back at Silver Sparrow. Neither of them looked threatening. At all.

Kris seemed kind of depressed, like he'd wanted Silver Sparrow to be more excited about crime-fighting. There was an awkward silence, so Sparrow went back to slurping up noodles one at a time. His slurping got louder and louder, and when Kris still didn't crack a smile, Sparrow said, "Check it out. I learned a new superpower."

He took one of the longest noodles, pushed the end of it under his silver beak, and shoved it up his nose. Then he opened his mouth, and after several choking sounds, pulled the other end of the noodle out from the back of his throat.

Kris and I immediately started gagging.

"Awww, quit it! Nooooo! That's *disgusting!*" Kris yelled, but he was doubled over, laughing and punching the seat of the van.

Silver Sparrow grinned and stuck out his tongue, one end of the noodle hanging out of his nose and the other out of his mouth.

It *was* disgusting. But I was laughing, too. How could you *not*?

"How old are you?" I asked, gasping for air.

"Eighth grade," Silver Sparrow said.

"*Eighth grade?* I thought you were in high school!"

He shrugged. "I'm big for my age." Then he made another gagging, gulping sound, and both ends of the noodle disappeared down his throat. He rubbed his stomach while Kris and I rolled in our seats in agony.

"Yummy yum yum," Silver Sparrow said. Eighth grade seemed about right. My cheeks hurt from laughing.

"Rein it in back there," Ekta called out as the minivan slowed down. "Mission starts now!"

Aunt Willow swiveled in her seat.

"ZZ!" She grinned and lifted her mask on top of her head so I could see the full-on look of wonder and happiness on her face. "An hour ago, I didn't know they existed, but I think I've *always* wanted to join a league of Real-Life Superheroes! Haven't you?"

I wasn't sure about the whole superhero thing, but hanging out with Willow all day and goofing around, laughing with new friends?

"Sure," I said. "Always."

BLANKETS

Crystal Warrior pulled the minivan into the parking lot of a nursing home and turned off the engine. From what Kris had told me, she'd heard from a friend's grandma that the home was shutting down, so she'd called up out of the blue and asked them to donate all their blankets to the Reality Shifters—her league of Real-Life Superheroes who were out to change the world.

Kris said the person on the phone thought it was a prank, but Crystal Warrior gave them one of her speeches. It was September in Maine and the nights were getting cold. The world *needed* heroes like the soon-to-be-former receptionist of the Wildwood Home for Seniors. *He*, former-receptionist man, could make sure every person experiencing homelessness in Port City had a way to keep warm at night. Generosity was a *superpower*.

In front of the building, next to several giant rolling carts full of blankets, a muscular silver-haired man in a navy-blue short-sleeved shirt, bright orange bike gloves, a blue eye mask, and an orange-and-blue-striped wheelchair was laughing and waving his hands at us.

I could feel the whole minivan drop lower as the side door opened and a ramp began to unfold. Papa Wheelie's biceps bulged as he wheeled toward us.

"Crystal, *how* many blankets did you order? I don't know if we can fit them all in here." Papa Wheelie chuckled and peered into the van. "Who's this? New recruits?"

"Couple of strays your niece picked up," Ekta said. "Don't get used to them. They're probably one-timers."

Papa Wheelie gave us a salute. "You'll learn this pretty quick about Crystal Warrior," he said. "She doesn't do anything halfway. You know we'll probably only need fifty of these, max, right?"

There were *two hundred* blankets.

We stacked them in the back of the minivan. We shoved them under and in between the seats. In the wayback, Wrecking Ball, Silver Sparrow, and I held still while superheroes piled at least a dozen heavy wool blankets high on each of our laps.

When all two hundred blankets had been crammed into the van, Crystal Warrior helped strap in Papa Wheelie and we headed for the parking lot outside City Hall to get organized.

Once there, Crystal Warrior handed us sunscreen and protein bars while Ocean distributed backpacks filled with bottled water and individually wrapped sandwiches.

"Make sure to drink water yourself," Ocean told me. "The last thing we need is some kid fainting while we're trying to save the planet."

I wasn't sure giving people blankets counted as "saving the planet," and I wasn't exactly clear about why we were handing all this stuff out and not bringing it to a shelter or a soup kitchen—which would be a *lot* easier—but I sipped some water and stuck close to Aunt Willow as the Reality Shifters went over their plan. They wanted to cover two large sections of the downtown, so the group would have to split up. Papa Wheelie, Silver Sparrow, and Crystal Warrior would cover the newer side—the Commercial District. Wrecking Ball, Ocean, Willow, and I would head in the opposite direction—toward historic City Center Square. And we'd all come back to the minivan when we ran out of supplies.

With backpacks slung over our shoulders and arms full of blankets, Willow and I followed the superheroes onto the sidewalk.

The staring started immediately. People stopped. Pointed. Laughed. Some of them even talked to us.

"It's a bird! It's a plane! It's *Superman!*"

"What's going on? Is there a parade today?"

"Woo-woo, check out the Fantastic Four!"

It was so embarrassing. With all those people staring at us, I was glad I had a mask and a stack of blankets to hide behind.

I walked closer to Wrecking Ball. "I thought you said we were invisible," I whispered.

"I meant they don't *see* us. They don't get what we're doing," he said. "Mom and Crystal have a new plan to change that, though. Publicity during day patrol."

"Publicity?" I asked.

"Crystal went to this summer youth group thing through her school and now she's all fired up about 'sound bytes' and 'messaging.'" Kris made air quotes with his fingers, but he looked excited about the plan. "She thinks maybe we could get on TV."

He nodded toward Ocean, who was stopping and talking to everyone.

"We're Real-Life Superheroes," she said. "The Reality Shifters. We're out here patrolling the area. Bringing hope to the hopeless, help to the helpless. Making Port City a better place. For *every* individual."

It was the same speech every time, and Ocean wasn't nearly as good as Crystal Warrior at delivery. *Hopeless* and *helpless* didn't have the same urgency when she said them.

In fact, they sort of sounded strange. Like Ocean wasn't 100 percent sold on that part of Crystal's speech. Most people nodded and walked right by. More than a few sped up their pace.

Two teenagers stopped to ask a bunch of questions like: "Who would win in a fight: Batman or Black Panther? What's better: invisibility or superstrength?"

Wrecking Ball answered those (Black Panther and invisibility) while Ocean shifted her blankets to one arm and gave a business card to their dad.

"Whoa, you have business cards," the guy said, eyeing us like he thought we might be trying to sell him something. He nudged the teenagers away and muttered something not-so-nice-sounding under his breath.

"He was rude," Willow said.

He *was* rude. But part of me didn't totally blame him. What we were doing felt kind of . . . weird. Even if it was helpful to give out blankets and food, why did we have to do it in costume?

Ocean shook her head. "That's what happens when you shake things up. Not everybody's going to like it. But you have to do something extreme to get people's attention these days. That's why we're out here, right?"

"It is?" I thought the mission was to help people without homes stay warm.

"You're going to *notice* someone in a superhero costume," Wrecking Ball said. "Our job is to get them to see why we're here."

"Exactly," Ocean said. "There are real problems in our city—homeless shelters are overfull, social services are overwhelmed, housing costs are through the roof—but most people want to pretend everything's fine. Maybe we inspire a few of them to wake up, take the blinders off, and *do* something about it."

"You're, like . . . shining a light!" Willow said.

Ocean laughed. "Yeah, but I want it to be a floodlight, not a flashlight."

I hadn't thought about it like that. I decided to try shining some superhero light. I lifted my chin and stopped avoiding the stares. The next time someone stopped to talk—it was a crabby woman in yoga pants—I hit her with a superhero smile.

"Good lord, this city is full of weirdos," the woman said.

I tried to stand tall, like Ocean, and not let it bug me. This woman and others like her weren't looking at me, I told myself. They were looking at the light.

CITY CENTER

The wool blankets were heavier than I'd expected. By the time we walked the three blocks to the large cobblestone plaza called City Center Square, my arms ached and my hands were sweating inside my elbow-length superhero gloves. The bottles of water in my backpack started to feel like they were filled with lead. Ocean was right. I was a one-timer. I wasn't cut out for this.

"Water up!" Ocean set her stack of blankets on the cobblestones next to a larger-than-life concrete statue of a lobsterman. She stretched her arms and took a swig from her bottle.

Gratefully, Willow and I dropped our blankets next to hers, but Wrecking Ball kept walking.

"I'm going to go talk to Jack," he said.

I sipped my water and watched as Wrecking Ball carried his blankets toward an old man leaning against the wall near the doorway of Mitsy's Diner. I wouldn't have even noticed the man. With all the people walking around—busy-looking men and women, families with strollers, teenagers on skateboards—he was practically invisible.

Wrecking Ball sat down cross-legged on the ground, unzipped his backpack, and handed over some water and sandwiches. Even across the square, I could see the man sit up straighter. He clasped his hand on Wrecking Ball's shoulder. Laughed. Like they were old friends.

"There are quite a few people living outdoors in this square," Ocean said. "And others who come and go. There are good awnings and insets to the buildings that are helpful when the weather's bad."

The radio station Dad works for is kitty-corner from Mitsy's Diner, but when Mom and I came to meet him for lunch, we usually tried not to notice anyone sleeping on benches or leaning against the walls. Even if they talked to us. Especially if they talked to us. It was like Ocean said: blinders.

She scooped up her blankets and waved her hand to the left. "You two are in charge of that side of the square. Never leave your buddy."

I looked at Willow. Wrecking Ball was far away from us, sitting next to Jack and the bags.

"Doesn't Kr—Wrecking Ball need a buddy?" I asked.

Ocean sighed and handed us each a whistle to hang around our necks. "You'll learn the ropes—if you don't quit on us tomorrow, which you probably will—but today, you're newbies. If you need help or if you see anyone who's in immediate trouble, blow this. I'll be there, lightning speed."

As Willow and I walked toward the radio station, it felt like I was looking at the square for the first time. Paying attention in a completely new way. Instead of thinking about where I was going, or focusing on all the moving people who were hurrying from one place to the next, I started to look for the people who were staying still. Like the white-haired woman sitting on a bench next to a shopping cart filled with bottles and cans. She wore an orange vest and blinked cloudy blue eyes at us as we approached.

I was nervous, but I tried to look extra-friendly behind my mask. I held out a blanket, imagining how glad she'd be to have it. How much warmer she'd be in the middle of the night. The woman in the vest looked at my outstretched blanket like it was infested with lice.

"No!" she said, mosquito-swatting the air. "I don't want your junk!"

I flinched, but Willow smiled and took a sandwich and a bottle of water out of her bag. "Are you thirsty? I'm Willow. What's your name?"

The woman took both items. Then threw them on the ground. The plastic bottle landed with a *thump* and rolled under the bench.

"Oh! Sorry," Willow breathed.

I wanted to reach out and hold Willow's hand, but my arms were full of blankets. I felt sorry for bothering the woman and a little mad at the same time. That was perfectly good water and food. Why didn't she want them?

"Hey! Rainbow Brite! I'll take a couple of those."

It took me a minute to remember I was wearing my rainbow leggings, and it took me a second more to find the voice that was shouting at me. A young man with tightly cropped black curls leaned against the wall on the stairs of the building where Dad worked. He looked like he was Willow's age.

I glanced at my aunt. It was hard to tell what she was thinking with her mask on.

"How do we know if he needs it?" I whispered. Our stuff was supposed to be for people who didn't have anything. Like the lady on the bench. This guy wore a Red Sox baseball cap and a clean black T-shirt and jeans. He seemed like he was doing okay.

Willow shrugged. "If he's cold, he's cold. It's not like we have a shortage of blankets."

The guy waved us over with one arm, and as we got closer I could see he had a thick scar across the bottom of his dark brown chin. I tried not to stare at it, but he caught me looking. He pointed a finger at his jaw and winked at me.

"Shark attack," he said.

I was pretty sure he was joking.

"I'm Derek," he said. He took two blankets off the stack in my arms and tossed them on top of an olive-green duffel bag at his feet. "You two join up with the superheroes?"

He looked at me, not Willow, but I wasn't sure how to answer. I mean, we'd joined up today, but was Willow planning to *actually* join up? Like, for real?

"We've got some sandwiches." Willow set down her blankets and unzipped her backpack. "Do you want one?"

"Yeah, thanks." Derek took the sandwich from Willow's outstretched hand. He sat down on the blankets and nodded toward the bottles of water inside her open backpack.

"Mind if I have one of those, too?"

"Oh. Right. Sorry." Willow handed him a bottle, then

zipped up her backpack and picked up her blankets. I figured that was it. We'd walk away. But the guy kept talking.

"What's your moniker? You got superhero names? Your
costumes could use some work. I mean, to be honest,
they're kinda . . . sad!"

He laughed a startling, happy laugh, and Willow laughed,
too. I couldn't help thinking about Mom and how much she
would freak out if she knew I was talking to strangers. All
those extra lives she'd saved up in her real-life city-walk
video game would simultaneously explode into one ginor-
mous game-over. Normally, I wouldn't even *think* about
answering this guy's questions. But I'd done so many strange
things already, I'd almost stopped feeling like myself. I felt
my mouth open and a bunch of words came out.

"We don't have names, yet. And these aren't our real
costumes. This is our first day out."

I said it like we actually *were* going to join the Reality
Shifters.

Derek raised his eyebrows and gave Willow a conspira-
torial grin. "Your first day? *No.* Really? You guys seem like
pros."

I was pretty sure he was joking again.

Derek swallowed a bite of sandwich and nodded toward
a concrete pillar near the street.

"See that bald white guy over there?"

We nodded. A sunburned man leaned against the pillar, holding a sign that said GO HOME!

"Don't mess with Gerry. Let Ocean handle him . . . or what's that other name she's trying? Panther-something?"

"Panthalassa," I said.

"Yeah, tell her I said that name's too complicated. And don't worry about Mary. She's all right."

"Who's Mary?"

Derek pointed in the direction of the old lady who'd yelled at us. She was eating the sandwich she'd thrown on the ground and the water bottle was sitting next to her on the bench, half-empty.

"She said she didn't *want* that . . ." I started, and Derek smiled.

"Wrecking Ball usually leaves her *two* sandwiches. Don't say anything to Mary, though. It makes her uncomfortable. Act like you dropped it. Maybe accidentally lose a blanket on your way out of here, too."

"Okay," I said. "Thanks." I was glad for the tip. I'd felt mad at Mary for throwing our stuff, but I didn't know anything about her. It wasn't fair to jump to conclusions.

"Always happy to help out a newbie RLSH." That surprised me. For everything Kris had said about people not noticing them, this guy seemed to know a lot about the Reality Shifters.

Derek went back to eating his sandwich, but as Aunt Willow and I turned to leave, he cleared his throat.

"Hey, Rainbow Brite." His smile disappeared and his voice got quiet. "I've got a mission for you, okay?"

BONI'S BAKERY

The closer we got to the Italian bakery, the slower I walked.

"Do you think we should whistle for Ekta? I mean Ocean?" I asked, gripping the bus pass Derek had given me. My arm-length gloves were too big, and even though the air was a little cool, my hands were sweating. It was hard not to drop the small slip of paper.

"Maybe," Willow said. "Let's check it out first. Assess the situation. These blankets are heavy, huh?"

I'd dropped one of mine when we passed by Mary's bench. I had to force myself not to look back to see if she'd picked it up. I should have dropped two.

"How do we know he's not . . . making it up? Or . . ." My voice trailed off.

I'd spotted the stairwell near Boni's Bakery. Dad loves working in City Center because there are all kinds of old-fashioned things about it, like the chunky cobblestones below our feet, and the fact that the whole square is blocked off for pedestrians only. He likes to talk about how some of the buildings, like the one where Boni's Bakery was, had been built in the 1800s and that's why, if you looked closely, lots of them had some odd details. Gargoyles. Hidden stained-glass windows. Roses made out of stone. Next to the bakery, there was a narrow iron stairwell cut into the building that led to nothing. No door. Just ten steps leading up to a solid brick wall.

Derek told us that earlier he'd seen someone on those steps. Someone new, who looked like she might need help. He said if she was still there, we should ask her if she wanted his bus pass. I'd memorized the words he'd written on the back: *Safe Harbor Women's Shelter, 52 Scarlet, route 1, 2nd stop.*

"Why didn't *you* give it to her?" I'd asked, but he shook his head.

"She wouldn't talk to me," he said. "I think she was scared. I was going to check on her again in a bit but . . . You two might have better luck. You know. Since you're superheroes and all."

His lips curled up, teasing us again.

"Did they give you the handbook?" he joked. "*How to Be a Superhero in Ten Easy Steps?*"

I *wished* I had a handbook. How were we supposed to know what to do? In the stairwell next to the bakery, a young woman with straight brown hair and a long skirt sat on the top step with a bundle in her lap. Willow and I stepped close to the stairs, but the second she caught us looking at her, the woman hugged the bundle closer and looked away.

If she didn't want the bus pass from Derek, why would she take it from us? How did we even know giving it to her was a good thing to do? Maybe what she really wanted was for everyone to leave her alone. Mom said sometimes the right thing to do was nothing at all. What if that was true now?

A man in a suit walked out of Boni's with a box that smelled amazing. He took a sharp right, checking his phone, and almost ran me over.

"Sorry." The guy looked up from the screen and did a double take before hurrying past. "Halloween already?" he mumbled. It was only for a split second, but when he looked up at me, I saw him glance around and lock eyes with the young woman on the stairs. He didn't stop or try to help, but he *saw* her. Just like Ocean said. Because of our light.

"I'm going to be a princess for Halloween."

A small voice drifted from some bushes next to the stairwell.

Willow sucked in her breath and nudged me with her elbow. A little girl, maybe six years old, peeked her head out from under a hedge and waved at us.

"Pearl!" The woman on the stairs stood up and tried to walk down toward the kid, but something was wrong. The minute she put weight on her right foot, she sucked in her breath and sat back down on the steps. The bundle in her arms started to cry.

"Are you okay?" Willow dropped her blankets next to my feet and took the stairs two at a time. "Do you need help?"

"No, no. I'm fine." But the woman didn't look fine. Even from the bottom of the stairs, I could see that her tanned arm was all scraped up and she was using her hair to hide a red blotch on her face. Either she'd fallen or someone had hurt her. Either way, it didn't look good. The baby in her lap kept crying.

"My sister cries too much," Pearl said to me. She'd been inching her way out from the hedge, and now she stood right next to me. "I like your mask. Are you a superhero?"

"Sort of," I said. "I like your tutu."

The girl did a spin until she got so dizzy that she stumbled. I pushed my stack of blankets next to her, and she flopped into them with an exaggerated "Oof!" Even the woman on the stairs smiled.

"I'm Willow, and this is my niece, Zinnia." Willow didn't ask the woman's name. Probably because, like me, she didn't expect the question to go over any better than it had with Mary. But after a beat, this woman said, "I'm Johanna," and scooted over to make room for Willow to sit next to her on the step. "Why are you dressed like that?" she asked.

"Well . . ." Willow looked suddenly embarrassed. "We're out here to help the . . ." she started to say Crystal Warrior's publicity line about helping the helpless, but paused, and I was glad she did. It didn't seem appropriate, somehow. This woman was hurt, but she didn't look helpless. She looked like she had her hands full. She quieted the baby and waited for my aunt to finish her sentence.

"Look," Willow said. "If you need anything . . . if you need somewhere to go . . ."

I tentatively held up the bus ticket. "Derek said you might want to go to Safe Harbor," I said. "You can have his bus ticket. If you want it. You don't have to take it."

Johanna bit her lip. Pearl was doing somersaults from my stack of blankets to Willow's and back again, and the static electricity was making her brown hair stick up all over the place. It was impossible not to laugh.

"I've been thinking about that place," Johanna said. "It's probably my best option, but it's way on the other side of town. The bus . . . with these kids . . . and . . ." She nodded toward her foot. "It's a lot." She bounced the baby on her good leg and sized Aunt Willow up. "You don't have a car, do you?"

"*They* do," I said. I scanned City Center until I spotted two spandex bodysuits at the far end of the square. I pointed them out to Johanna and Pearl and held up my whistle. "I can call them over. I bet they'll drive you. If you want."

"Superheroes!" Pearl said, and sat very still, staring in the direction of Ocean and Wrecking Ball.

Johanna looked worried and was quiet for a while, but eventually she kissed the baby's head, then nodded. "Yeah, okay. Thanks."

I didn't want to scare Pearl, so I sat down on the blanket next to her. "Do you like whistles?" I asked.

I blew two short, friendly tweets, then handed the whistle over. Pearl kneeled on the blankets and blew her lungs out until everyone around us started staring a little *too* much and I had to take the whistle away.

It wasn't exactly lightning speed, but close enough. When Ocean and Wrecking Ball showed up, Ocean called the shelter to see if they had space and then offered to call a taxi, which made Johanna's shoulders instantly relax. If she'd been having second thoughts about getting in a car with a bunch of costumed strangers, I couldn't blame her. I'd felt the same way. I sat on the blankets and played patty-cake with Pearl until the car came. Any doubts I'd had about Derek and his mission had vanished. Not only had he seen a person in trouble, he knew exactly what she needed, and he knew she would trust us more than she would trust him. If anyone was a superhero today, it was Derek.

The driver of the taxi was a nice woman who promised to help Johanna to the door when they got there. Pearl wouldn't get in the car until she'd high-fived all four of us. Except when she got to me, she threw her arms around my waist. Her small, bony limbs felt stronger than you expected them to, like Wally's used to feel when he jumped on your back for a ride. It took my breath away.

"What kind of superheroes are you?" Pearl asked me.

I looked at Willow and felt a smile creeping into my lips.

"Reality Shifters," I said. "We're *Real-Life* Superheroes."

Pearl nodded. "I'm going to be a Reality Shifter for Halloween," she said. "Or maybe a princess. I don't know."

"It's okay," I said. "Either one of those would be great."

Ocean clapped her hand on my shoulder as the taxi

drove away. "That was good work, girls," she said. "You made a real difference in the world today."

"Nice job, Zin," Wrecking Ball said, and held out his fist for a bump.

I don't know how it happened, but suddenly, I felt lighter. Like a balloon was inflating inside my chest, lifting me off the ground. Seeing Pearl and her family get in that taxi, on their way to a safe place, made me want to skip all the way back to the van. And later, after we'd finished giving out our stacks of blankets and my muscles were dead-tired like I'd walked twenty miles, I did. My legs were wobbly and my feet were sore, but I skipped down the sidewalk anyway. Aunt Willow skipped with me, laughing and singing some old jazz song about blue skies. We were almost to the parking lot when Ocean stopped for one final mission.

"Wait!" she barked, and halted in front of a steaming pile of dog poo.

"Gross," Wrecking Ball said.

Instead of steering us around it, Ocean whipped a plastic bag out of the pocket of her backpack and scooped up the pile.

It kind of blew my mind. All the times Mom and I had avoided poo on the street, it had seemed inevitable. An annoying pitfall that everyone had to put up with. It might seem silly, but it never occurred to me you could *do* something about it. That you could see a problem and in one simple move, you could make a change for the better.

Ocean smirked when she caught me staring at her. "I told you it wasn't all glitz and glamour. Superheroes take care of the small, stinky stuff, too."

As she looked around for the nearest trash can, I took the bag out of her hand.

"I've got it," I said, and skipped ahead to throw it away. "Mission accomplished!"

The others were waiting for us when we got to the parking lot. The back of the minivan was still filled with most of the blankets, but we'd given out more than I'd thought. Papa Wheelie had returned to the van five times for more supplies and personally handed out thirty blankets, which was the record for the day. He looked hot and sweaty from all the effort, but he was grinning.

"Got a good workout!" he said, and he gave me a high five when Ocean told him that Willow and I had lasted the whole mission without running out of steam. It wasn't a great compliment, but the way she said it made it sound not too shabby.

"You should come again next Saturday," Wrecking Ball said.

"Ka-*kaw!*" Sparrow agreed.

Willow and I both looked at Ocean and Crystal Warrior. I was surprised at how much I wanted them to say we could come.

Ocean shrugged. "It's supposed to rain. Think you can handle it?"

But Crystal Warrior touched the star sapphire at her neck and nodded straight at me.

"I *knew* you had a light inside of you," she said. "I could see it the moment we met."

And even though I knew that couldn't possibly be true—because the moment we met was *not* my brightest—I did feel a little glowy.

"We're in!" Willow said, and her smile was a full-on flood-light. It lit me up. Not only because we'd been invited back, but because next Saturday was a whole week away. Which meant Aunt Willow was going to stay.

SPECTRUM

That night before bed, I scanned the stack of empty journals on my bedside table and brought one of them to my sleeping bag on the floor. I'd chosen a bright red blank book with a happy-faced sun on the cover. A speech bubble hovered above the sun: *Make the world brighter, one ray at a time!* It seemed appropriate.

I cracked the book open, clicked my pen, and got so absorbed I almost didn't notice that the voices in the kitchen had gotten louder. When Willow came to bed, her eyes were red and puffy. Maybe she was just tired, but from my spot on the floor, it looked like she'd been crying.

"You okay?" I asked. I wondered briefly if she'd told Mom and Dad about the superheroes, but I knew Willow wouldn't say anything. We'd promised each other we wouldn't breathe a word. At least not right away. Ekta said RLSH don't have to keep their superhero names and identities secret. But Kris said lots of them do, including him. For the fun of it. And so people don't bother them.

"Your mom wants me to go back to school."

"Are you going to?"

"No."

I let out my breath. I hadn't realized I'd been holding it in.

"What are you going to do?" I asked.

Willow flopped onto my bed and stared up at the stars on my ceiling for so long that I thought maybe she hadn't heard the question. Or maybe she was ignoring me. But then she turned on her side and smiled.

"I'm going to think of a really good superhero name."

I smiled back and unzipped myself from my sleeping bag so I could hand her the blank book I'd been writing in. I'd crossed out all the ideas I didn't like and put stars and hearts around the one remaining word.

~~Cygnus~~   ~~Swan Girl~~

~~Rainbow Brite~~   ~~Bright Star~~

~~Super Star~~   ~~Super Swan~~

~~Rainbow Girl~~   ~~Rainbow Spectrum~~

♡ **Spectrum** ✮ ♡
✮ ♡

At first, Willow was quiet, reading through all the options I'd come up with. I kind of wished I'd erased them. Or scratched them out darker so she wouldn't see.

"I almost forgot about Cygnus," she said. "Wally hated that story."

"No he didn't," I said. "Only the end. He liked the rest of it."

"Right. The exciting parts. Walleye always liked the exciting parts. *Captain* Walleye, I should say."

She grinned at me when she used my brother's nickname, but I didn't want to think about it. Walleye made me think of fish, which made me think of the lake and the dock. Which led to the tippy canoe and Wally's last Sunday at home. I felt kind of bad even thinking it, but I didn't want any of *that* to get mixed up with the day Willow and I had shared. Putting on costumes and being superheroes.

Cygnus the Swan was the first thing that popped into my mind when I'd opened that blank book, but there was a reason I'd crossed it out. Meeting the RLSH felt like the start of something *new*. And that newness felt like a warm, bright, sunny blanket of hope. Perfectly intact. Without a brother-shaped hole in it. It felt selfish to want to keep it that way, but I did.

"Those were fun. Our constellation nights," Willow said.

"Mm-hmm," I said, suddenly feeling exhausted. My arms ached from lugging around the heavy backpack and blankets. Finally, when I couldn't stand waiting anymore, I sucked in my breath and asked, "So? What do you think of it? My superhero name?"

Willow's eyes went back to the page.

"*Spectrum*," she said. The sound of it out loud made my ears tingle and I knew I'd made the right choice. "Like when you look at sunlight through a prism?"

"Right," I said. "When light gets separated into all the colors—the full spectrum—it's a rainbow."

"SPEC-*trum*." Willow said it again, with gravity, like an announcer in a movie trailer. It sounded strong and mysterious. "It's perfect, Z. It really is."

She put the journal on the nightstand and turned out the lamp. The glow-in-the-dark stars on my ceiling let off their dim, yellow light. I closed my eyes so I wouldn't see the cross-shaped constellation, Cygnus, hovering over my head. Even without looking, I knew where the five main stars were. The brightest star, Deneb, at the tail. The two wing stars reaching out to the right and left. The center star: the heart. The head was the smallest and faintest, placed far from the rest, like the swan was extending his neck. Stretching it as far as he could. Craning. Searching.

There were lots of stories about Cygnus, but that was the one Willow always told. The one where his friend Phaethon steals the sun chariot and races it across the sky until he gets hit by Zeus's lightning. Phaethon falls out of the chariot, plunges into the river, and Cygnus dives in to save his friend. He dives and he dives, but he can't find Phaethon. So he keeps diving. His sadness fills the river, but he doesn't stop. He dives until his neck stretches out long. He cries until he loses his voice. His waterlogged fingers grow webs and his arms get pinned to his side. Even when white feathers hide his hair and massive white wings cover his back. Still. He won't give up.

Finally, Zeus sees how much love and sadness Cygnus has in his heart, and he pulls him out of the water. But Cygnus isn't a human anymore. He's a swan. Zeus places him in the sky, and that heart, so full, starts to burn. The love and sadness inside it transform into hydrogen and helium. A fiery mass of gas. A star. Another for his tail. Two more for his wings. But Cygnus stretches his neck as far as he can before he's completely pinned in place. Searching. Forever.

That was the part Wally hated. That Cygnus was stuck. It didn't matter that the swan was immortal. Or that Cygnus reminded people about love every time they looked at the stars. My brother didn't care about that.

"New story," he'd say. Only he didn't want a new story. He wanted to hear about Cygnus again. But with a different ending.

FEATHERS

"I'm thinking about *Spectrum*," I announced.

Language Arts was the only class I had with Kris, so it was the first time I'd seen him since our Saturday mission. It made me smile, thinking about how less than forty-eight hours ago, we'd been in superhero costumes. Helping people. Making a difference. Changing lives. And no one in this room had any idea.

On Sunday, I'd turned eleven, and I honestly felt different. Most of the time, birthdays are fun, you have cake and a few presents, but nothing really *changes*. But this year, I felt stronger and taller, like I'd grown another three inches over the weekend and I didn't even mind.

Class hadn't started yet, and nothing was happening. Mr. Iftin was writing on the board, but Kris's eyes were glued to the front of the room. Like watching the words *Journal entries due Friday . . .* appear on the whiteboard was the most fascinating thing he'd ever seen.

"It's like Rainbow, but more serious." I stepped closer to his desk, trying to get his attention. "I thought maybe for my cos—"

"Zinnia!" Kris didn't say it, he coughed it. The cough sounded so real, I wasn't even sure he'd said my name. He still wasn't looking at me, but he shook his head slightly and tapped a finger on his lips. The motion was quick, like brushing off a crumb, but I knew he meant I should zip it.

"Oh! Sorry," I said, getting the picture. He wanted to stay inconspicuous. Undercover. "I didn't know—"

"You didn't know what? That you lost *this*?"

Trevor's voice behind me made me cringe. Miraculously, I'd been able to avoid him all day. He'd gotten pulled out of second period and didn't show up again until halfway through Science, at which point Ms. Bekker had already paired me with someone else for this week's project. It was like I'd been given new powers—a shield of self-preservation.

But now, Trevor reached toward me and pretended to take something out of my back pocket. My reflexes kicked in. I yelped. Jumped out of the way. And tripped over the leg of a chair.

My hands grabbed Kris's desk for balance and I acciden-tally knocked all his books on the floor. They landed with an explosive *slap!*

Everyone in the classroom, including Mr. Iftin, turned to watch as Trevor waved a giant peacock feather in my face. Three. Feet. Tall. The opposite of inconspicuous.

The room went silent as the wispy green edges of the feather vibrated in the air. An iridescent spot at the top stared at me like a deep blue extremely shiny eye. Around the blue was a circle of turquoise. Then a rim of green. Orange. Yellow-green. It was almost like a rainbow.

"You should keep it," Trevor said, grinning. "I mean, it came out of your *tail feathers* anyway. So . . . happy birthday!"

Some kids behind us snickered, and I didn't even have time to wonder how Trevor Pryor knew my birthday because pretty soon there was so much whispering and laughing about "tail feathers" that Mr. Iftin had to clap his hands to settle everyone down.

The only color missing from the feather was red, and my face made up for that. The fire spread from my ears to my cheeks and down my neck. I glimpsed Anji and Jade, holding their hands to their mouths, eyes wide with either shock or hilarity. I was certain they were laughing at me.

The tall, strong feeling I'd had a moment ago evaporated. I slunk low in my chair, back to wishing I could shed an inch or three.

Trevor, on the other hand, looked completely satisfied with himself. He smiled as he placed the feather on my desk and moved toward his own at the back of the room. He helped Kris pick up his books on his way.

"What were you talking to Zinnia about?" Trevor asked.

Kris slammed a book on the table and frowned at me.

"We weren't talking," he said.

I barely heard anything that came out of Mr. Iftin's mouth for the first ten minutes of class. Out of all the people in the entire school, why did Trevor insist on torturing *me*? I'd never done anything to him. Honestly. I racked my brain, running through the events of last semester in my mind. I couldn't come up with *one* motive Trevor Pryor would have for making me the butt of every single joke he ever invented.

I'd definitely *ignored* Trevor, but other kids were meaner to him than I was. Way meaner. Josh Pelletier once put him inside a locker and closed the door. The kind of classic bully move you'd see in an old movie. Which probably explained everything. It's not like Trevor could get back at Josh Pelletier. That kid ate mean for breakfast. So there had to be someone else, and I was the easiest target. The weakest link. In the animal documentary of life, I was the sad little gazelle with the limp that the herd leaves behind.

The strong, eleven-year-old feeling was dead. Worse. It was like it never existed. I slunk deeper into my chair and glared at the peacock feather on my desk, letting my eyes unfocus so the rainbow colors blurred together. But I sat back up again when I realized kids were moving around. Jade and Anji were hugging, and from the back of the room, Trevor was heading my way. Slowly, my brain processed the last two terrifying words Mr. Iftin had said:

"Pair up!"

Trevor grinned at me like this was the opportunity he'd been waiting for all day. Like the tail feather was only the beginning of a brand-new store of poultry-related material he'd been saving up over the weekend.

Kris had his head down, drawing on his notebook.

"Be my partner," I whispered.

He didn't answer. Maybe he didn't hear me.

"Please be my partner?" I begged. "Pleasepleaseplease."

"Wait a minute!" Mr. Iftin called out. "There's an odd number. We'll need one group of three."

It was the opening I needed, and in my head, it worked out perfectly. I raised my hand. Stood up. In a loud, firm voice, I announced, *I'll join Jade and Anji.* And instead of laughing the chicken-girl out of the classroom, they hopped out of their seats and squashed me in a three-person hug.

But in real life, I didn't say anything. Trevor sat down in the desk behind me. He leaned over to Kris, and said, "You're the odd man out. Want to join Team Chicken?"

It wasn't great. But at least it was better than being with Trevor on my own.

That's when Kris raised his hand. Looked steadily at Mr. Iftin, and announced in a loud, firm voice, "I work better on individual projects." He picked up his books. "I'll do mine on my own."

Then he moved to Trevor's deserted desk in the back corner of the room.

Mr. Iftin went back to the board and wrote, *How to . . . Write a How-To Article.*

Trevor shot me an evil grin. "Let's talk turkey."

HOW-TO

"How to . . . *build a chicken coop*? How to . . . *scramble eggs*? What else? Butchering? Too gross? We could do it like a horror show. That could be hilarious." Trevor started making screeching noises and pretended to stab the air over my head with an invisible knife. I felt pinned to my chair. I froze. And the more horrified I looked, the faster and louder the imaginary stabbing got until Mr. Iftin showed up at my desk.

"How're we doing over here?" he asked.

"Great!" Trevor paused mid-stab and grinned like he was having the time of his life. "We're going to write our how-to article about how to butcher chickens."

Mr. Iftin made his face relax into his no-judgment-I'm-listening look.

"And how do *you* feel about that, Zinnia?"

"It's fine," I said. Even though it wasn't. Even though I wanted to do *anything* but write a how-to article with Trevor Pryor.

Especially not about chickens.

Getting stabbed.

"Well, it's a *start*." Mr. Iftin put his hand gently on Trevor's still-raised fist until Trevor loosened his grip on the fake dagger and his hand dropped to his lap. "Why don't you take one more pass through the brainstorming stage? Try this: Five minutes of silent effort. I want each of you to make two lists. Things you know a *lot* about and things you want to know *more* about. Then compare and see if you can agree on an even *better* idea."

"But we want to write about—" .

"Just try it." Mr. Iftin gave Trevor a serious-warning look, then smiled. "It's the genius of brainstorming. The best ideas are usually buried underneath the obvious ones. Besides, you've got time. We'll be working on this project all month. You want to come up with something you won't get tired of researching."

All *month*?

"Five minutes. Two lists. Starting . . . *now*." Mr. Iftin checked his watch and headed back to his desk.

Trevor shrugged and started scribbling in his notebook. I was glad that the game of stabby charades was over. But *a month*? This was probably all part of the Pryor Master Plan. He'd distracted me with the feather fiasco and now I was stuck working on a monthlong project with him. As if he didn't already have enough opportunities to make my life miserable. I stared at my blank page and wished I had a time machine I could hop into and leap ahead thirty days.

"Don't think too much, Zinnia," Mr. Iftin called from the front of the room. "Write down whatever pops into your head and don't stop. I want to see that pencil moving."

I tried to turn off my brain. No thinking, just writing. Fine. I was tired of thinking anyway. I put my pencil to the page and started a list. *Things I Know a Lot About. Stars. Light. Snails. Rainbows. Moving. Loneliness. Cancer.*

I scribbled out the last two and moved on to the next list. *Things I Want to Learn More About.*

"*That!*"

Trevor reached over and pounded his finger on the words I'd just written: *Real-Life Superheroes.*

"*That's* what we're doing," he said. "Mr. Iftin was right. It's a way better idea. Besides, look!"

He pushed his own notebook toward me and slammed his finger on the page. In his *Things I Know a Lot About* column, he'd written *Superheroes.*

"It's true," he said. "I know everything about super-heroes. I've got five hundred and fifty-two comics at home.

Most were my dad's. Do you *actually* think there are super-heroes in real life?"

I bit my lip. The good news was that Trevor, for the first time I could remember, was *not* teasing me about feathers or clucking or laying eggs. Even his question about super-heroes seemed sincere. Not snarky. Not a setup designed to get everyone's attention and then throw me under the bus.

The bad news? I glanced toward the back of the room to see if Kris was listening, but he had his head down, his left arm curved around the paper he was writing on, as if he didn't want anyone to see. Not that a single person was looking. Kris was so good at being invisible.

I *knew* he wanted me to keep the Reality Shifters a secret. Stay undercover. Inconspicuous. He clearly didn't want me telling Trevor Pryor or anyone else at school his secret identity. The question was: Would he be mad if I wrote about the RLSH in *general*? Not *his* team, just the idea? I wouldn't be spilling any secrets. I'd be writing a generic how-to assignment. That only Mr. Iftin, Trevor, and I would see.

There wasn't really an option. I had a project to get through, and Kris had abandoned me. No one in a spandex suit was going to rush to my rescue. I had to save myself.

"Okay, sure," I said. "We can write about that. They're called the RLSH."

MILES

Mom was getting ready for a shift at the café when I got home from school.

"Have you seen my apron?" she asked, checking her watch. "Your dad's out on assignment and won't be back until late. There's a pizza in the freezer for dinner."

"Okay," I said. I pulled Mom's Powerhouse Café apron out of the laundry basket I'd tripped over in the living room. "Where's Willow?"

Mom rolled her eyes. "She went to do some 'thinking.' Whatever that means."

"Oh. We were going to . . ." *Work on our costumes* was what I was going to say. I stopped myself and tried not to feel disappointed, but nothing gets past Mom.

"Do what?" But before I had time to come up with an

answer, Mom checked her watch again, annoyed. "I would never have said yes to the 3 P.M. shift if I thought you were going to be alone."

"You can go," I said. "I'll be fine."

Mom paused, narrowed her hawk eyes at me, and nudged me toward the kitchen table.

"Sit down a sec. I want to talk to you about something."

"You should go," I said, hoping to avoid whatever topic of conversation was making her eyebrows scrunch together. "I don't want you to be late."

"You *know* how Willow can be, right?"

I shook my head like I had no idea what she was talking about. Even though I knew exactly what she meant. *Unreliable. Disappointing.* But Willow seemed different this trip. We had a mission. We weren't going to sleepwalk through life. We were going to do something that mattered. Together. It wasn't Mom's fault she didn't know that yet. How could she? It was a secret.

Mom pressed her lips together like she was trying to figure out how to explain.

"Sometimes she promises things, and then doesn't—"

I looked at the clock. "I get it," I said. "It's all good. I'm fine. You should go."

She hesitated, then stood up slowly. "I want you to

keep the expectations low, okay? She'll be heading back to school soon anyway."

"You think so?" I wished I hadn't asked the question. I didn't want to hear her answer.

"I *know* so," Mom said. "I'm not sure what's going on with Willow right now, but she's going to figure it out and as soon as she does, she'll take off. Like she *should*. She's doing amazing at school. Hey . . ." She shook her head at my frown. "Look on the bright side—you'll get your room back. Call me if she's not here in ten minutes. I'll have someone come get you and you can hang out with me at the café."

Mom kissed me on the forehead and even after she shut the door behind her, I could feel the pressure of her lips, warm on my skin. I didn't want to let it sink in. Any of it. First of all, not sharing a room with Willow was the opposite of a bright side. And second of all, I didn't *want* to keep my expectations low. I wanted to believe in Aunt Willow. Believe that she came to Maine because she wanted to be here. With us. With me.

But then there was reality. We were supposed to be making costumes, and instead, I was home alone with a frozen pizza. I hated to admit, it was a classic Willow move. I wondered how many days I had left before my aunt packed up and went back to school.

"Oh my gosh, I thought she was never going to leave!" Willow burst through the front door, her arms full of bags from Goodwill. "I didn't want to come in with all this stuff because you *know* she'd start asking a million questions, so I had to sit and keep a lookout from your bench in the park. God, she should run the CIA or something, she is such a hawk!"

I busted out laughing, partly from relief and partly because that's the exact bird Dad and I always use to describe Mom. The same Mom, by the way, who'd been completely, irreversibly, 100 percent wrong about my aunt.

"What is all that?" I followed Willow into my bedroom— *our* bedroom—and watched as she dumped the Goodwill bags on the bed.

"Options!" Willow grinned. "We are going to make the best costumes the Reality Shifters have ever seen."

"Kris said they call them gimmicks, not costumes."

Willow's eyes sparkled. "Call it whatever you want. It. Is. ON! Now we just need some superhero music."

She plugged her phone into a speaker and immediately the room was filled with earsplitting, superfast trumpet music. It sounded like a bunch of frantic, out-of-tune chickens running around, punctuated by short, panicky drum solos.

"*Willow!*" I complained, but I was laughing.

"No, you're going to love this album, Z." Willow started sorting through the pile on the bed. "It's Miles Davis playing live at Newport. Old-school classic stuff. I need it for inspiration. It's part of my cos—gimmick. What do you think of this RLSH name?"

She grabbed a creased tweed hat with a black band off the pile on the bed and placed it on her head before spreading out her fingers and waving her hands through the air for the big reveal.

"*MILES!*"

It wasn't very superhero-ish. "Like, Miles Morales?" I'd seen the *Spider-Verse* movie, but Miles was Spider-Man's *alter ego*. The regular kid, not the superhero.

"I guess. Sure. And *Miles* Davis. Who was a music superhero. Plus, I flew *miles* to get here. And then there's the Robert Frost poem: . . . *miles to go before I sleep*. Which is pretty much my life. Perfect, right?"

She seemed to like it a lot, so I ignored my opinions about the name and the musical "superhero" we were listening to and said, "Definitely. Cool. Did Miles Davis wear a hat?"

"Maybe. I just like the look of the fedora. Don't you? I was originally thinking *this* . . ." She held up a long, flowy dress decorated with music notes. "But I think I want an old-school-detective look instead. Like film noir. How about you? What do you want your costume to be?"

I hadn't thought I'd be that interested in making a super-hero persona, but now that I had the perfect name, I threw myself into creating the perfect gimmick for Spectrum. Willow had brought home belts, gloves, scarves, suspenders, even a pair of butterfly wings "just in case." We tried every single item. Because you never know.

Surprisingly, after the first song, the Miles Davis music wasn't half bad. It was actually kind of bouncy and fun. Willow caught me tapping my toes and taught me a couple swing dance moves. We twirled and dipped until I tripped over her guitar case and couldn't get up off the floor because I was laughing so hard.

I forced myself not to think about the poem she'd quoted: *miles to go before I sleep.* I didn't want Miles to go anywhere.

GIMMICK

By the time the pizza was done cooking, I had my gimmick all worked out. It was really just the eye mask I'd gotten from Silver Sparrow plus a tricked-out version of my first-day-of-school outfit. Rainbow-striped leggings, Doc Martens, the black dress I'd gotten for Grandma's picture, and a wide red belt from the Goodwill stash.

At first, I didn't want to do it, but Willow spied the peacock feather sticking out of my backpack, and we cut off the top and glued the rainbow eye to the belt. I had to admit, it looked pretty cool.

For the finishing touch, we tried out a pair of bright red arm-length gloves that Willow said looked like they belonged at a fancy dinner party in the 1950s. The fingers were way too long, but they made the outfit look sleek and official, like a superhero in a blockbuster movie. I took the gloves off to shove a giant pepperoni slice into my mouth.

Willow was scrolling on her phone wearing her own black eye mask and the fedora. She had on fingerless black leather gloves, black pants with suspenders, a white button-down shirt, and a heavy black leather trench coat that smelled like mothballs and dust. She looked less like a superhero and more like a detective from an old black-and-white movie. With a mask over her eyes. I wasn't sure she was getting the whole superhero concept. But I didn't care. She looked great.

"Ohmuhgosh." Willow's mouth was full but she waved me over to look at her phone. "Did you know there's a Miles Davis album called *Panthalassa*? I mean, it's a remix album they made after he died. But still. That's wild. We've got to tell Ekta."

I moved closer as she tapped on the album cover and the room filled with a low hum, like the background music in a movie scene where the villain is around the corner, about to close in. Willow grinned and let the phone drop on the bed.

"Superhero music!"

The hum swelled and grew sinister, and Willow hopped to her feet, bending her knees in a fake attack stance. I pulled on my red gloves and faced her, grinning my head off.

"You'll never get past *Spectrum*!" I said in a proud super-hero voice.

Willow stretched out her right arm in a slow-motion punch and I blocked it with my superpowered red-gloved elbow. She tried the same move with her left arm and threw in a side kick. I dodged out of the way, my superboots leaping into action.

"Nice try!" I shouted. "But you're no match for my full-spectrum laser eyes!"

I squinted at her behind my mask, pretending to blast her with laser-equipped lenses. Willow fell backward, collapsed onto the bed, and the minute she hit the mattress, the music changed. Right on cue. Like there was a movie director arranging the whole thing. The second she fell, an electric guitar started to play over the villainous hum. A melody formed, slow and peaceful. Almost sad, like it was mourning my superhero aunt's tragic death by rainbow-laser eyes.

Willow's smile disappeared and she sucked in her breath in surprise.

"Are you okay?" I thought maybe she'd landed on a hanger or something sharp, but she shook her head.

"I know this song," she said. "The original version."

She reached to turn it off, but I stopped her.

"I like it," I said.

It was really beautiful. Nothing like the other Miles Davis songs we'd been listening to. It was soft and calm, but it had something haunting to it, too.

"What's it called?" I asked.

"'In a Silent Way.'" Willow's eyes drifted to her guitar case.

"You know how to play it?"

The second she nodded, I rushed over to plug in her amp. I hadn't heard Willow play once since she got to Maine. I unlocked her guitar case, plugged in the cable, and handed her the instrument. She shrugged off the smelly leather coat and started to play along. I lay down on my sleeping bag and let the sounds wash over me.

Willow started softly at first, matching the sounds of the guitar on the recording. Then she started playing higher notes that soared over the melody, blending and building on what was already there. I stared at my ceiling and couldn't help but think that *this* was exactly the song that should be the soundtrack for Cygnus the Swan. Diving. Searching. Feathers sprouting.

Then a trumpet joined in, clear and bright as a star. I was starting to feel like the music was sinking through my skin, soaking into my bones when suddenly, it stopped. Without warning, Willow unplugged her phone from the speaker and laid down the guitar.

"Wait!" I said. "It wasn't over. That was *amazing*."

But Willow shook her head. Even behind her superhero mask, I could see that her eyes were all shiny. She tipped the fedora forward to hide her face.

"It's too sad, Z. I can't play that one."

"Play me something else, then."

Willow *always* wanted to play guitar, but now she sighed. "Maybe later."

I felt the mood falling and I searched my brain, trying to come up with a joke or a funny story to make Willow laugh again. Anything to get that wet shine out of her eyes and bring her smile back into the room.

I stared out the window, searching for something. Anything. My view of the backyard was blocked by my rainbow curtains, pulled half closed.

"We need to make a rainbow cape," I said. "For Spectrum!"

Willow tilted her fedora back on her head. Her smile returned, lighting up the room.

"Yes." She nodded. "Yes, we do."

Mom worked the morning shift the rest of the week, and Dad didn't have any more evening assignments, so Willow and I had to wait until Friday after school to show our costumes to Ekta and Kris.

I was distracted all day. In the morning, I brought my math book to Social Studies and my social studies book to Math. At lunch, I was so out of it that I didn't even notice I was standing between Jade and Anji in the lunch line until Jade tapped me on the shoulder and handed me a note. I had been thinking about what Crystal Warrior would say about my gimmick and whether she'd notice that my peacock feather looked like an eye, just like her pink star stone.

I *knew* she was going to love the cape. It had turned out perfectly. It flowed over my shoulders and down to the back of my knees in full-spectrum rainbow glory. Willow had helped me sew a drawstring around the neck, and then, to keep Mom from being suspicious, we had to make new curtains out of the music-note dress that Willow had rejected for her Miles costume.

The curtains weren't pretty and they didn't exactly fit the windows, but Mom believed our story that we were on a redecorating kick. We only had to show her two online videos about DIY curtains and throw pillows before her eyes glazed over. That tactic was Willow's idea: distract and bore to tears. She's a genius.

Before I realized what I was doing, I'd opened Jade's note and read it:

Meet at the Ice Cream Shack after school?

I jerked back to reality. What was I doing? This note was supposed to be *passed*, not read. What kind of a person *reads* people's private notes? My ears burned as I tapped Anji on the shoulder and handed her the piece of paper.

"Here. Sorry," I breathed. Then, because they both looked sort of disappointed and shocked, and because I didn't know what else to do, I ducked out of line as fast as I could, mumbling something about having to pee. Which made the ear-burning worse.

"I could have come up with a less embarrassing lie," I told Willow after school. We were sitting in the rocking chairs on the porch, trying to act all low-key until Mom got her stuff together and left the house.

"Ice Cream Shack sounds great," Willow said. "You should ask if you can go with them sometime."

"Go where? With who?" Mom hurried out the screen door, shoving her apron in her bag while she headed for the porch stairs. "I'd want to meet their parents first. See you girls after my shift!"

We watched her walk down Ocean Avenue and turn the

corner toward Powerhouse Café. We sat ninety seconds more.

Calm.

Cool.

Collected—

As soon as we were *sure* she was gone, we bolted for our room and put on our gimmicks.

THE CAPE CONUNDRUM

I didn't expect Ekta and Kris to applaud or shriek with joy when they saw our gimmicks. But I thought they'd be way more enthusiastic than they were. The minute we stepped into the upstairs apartment, Kris smirked. Ekta full-on rolled her eyes.

"*Rookies*," she muttered.

I looked at Willow. Her eyes blinked behind her mask.

"You don't like them?" Willow asked.

Kris kept smirking.

"Here, quick!" Ekta pointed to the coffee table in the far corner of the living room. "Our lives are at stake unless Spectrum picks up that pencil and stabs the villain in fifteen seconds or less."

"Gross," I said. "I don't want to stab anyone."

"Don't worry," Kris said. "It's a training exercise. It'll never happen in real life."

Ekta held up a stopwatch. She was serious. "1 . . . 2 . . . *Go!*"

I turned my superboots toward the living room and took off like my life depended on it. I could feel my cape flowing behind me, the fate of the world on my shoulders. I reached for the pencil and estimated what my time would be. Six seconds? Five? I let myself fantasize about beating the RLSH world record for imaginary-villain pencil-stabbing.

Except I couldn't pick up the pencil. The too-long fingertips of my supergloves kept getting in the way. Twice, I missed the target altogether. The third time, I managed to clutch it in my hand, but lost control and the pencil rolled off the table. I lunged and felt the drawstring of my cape tighten around my neck. Someone had a grip on it. Not strong enough to choke me, but strong enough to let me know they could.

"Hey!" I reached for my throat, but of course I couldn't untie the string. Because of the gloves.

"And . . ." Ekta held my cape in one hand and clicked her stopwatch with the other. "We're dead."

My face burned.

Ekta let go of the rainbow cape and tugged on the back of Willow's black leather trench coat.

"Nice. Vintage. Thick. Similar hazard here, but you can wiggle out of it if you get caught. That's not your biggest problem."

"What's her biggest problem?" I asked, though I thought I knew some answers. Smelly leather. Detective, not superhero.

"Remember last weekend in City Center?" Ekta asked my aunt.

"Yeah?"

"How'd you feel carrying those blankets and backpacks?"

Willow shrugged. "Good?"

"Tired? Hot?"

"Oh. Yes." Willow's face was getting red, too.

"Okay, so with this coat, you've added extra weight and extra heat. And what do you get in exchange?"

"It *looks* cool?" Willow joked, but Ekta wasn't having it.

"*Seconds* can make a difference out in the field. Heat stroke can happen to anyone. We can't have individuals on our team putting themselves in danger. It's unnecessary, irresponsible, and it looks bad. This isn't cosplay. We're trying to *do* something here."

"I guess . . . I didn't think about it that way." Willow pushed her gloved hands into the pockets of her stinky coat. Neither of us had expected Kris and Ekta to take our clothes so seriously. As if they needed more proof that we weren't cut out for the RLSH.

"Also, those shoes and dress pants are made for sitting at a desk. They're going to inhibit you when you really need to move." Ekta picked up her cell phone and started dialing. "Where are you? We've got a cape conundrum," she said into the phone. Then to Willow, "Come with me."

She led Willow into the back bedroom, leaving me and Kris to stare at the pencil on the floor. Deflated, I pulled off my red gloves and untied the drawstring around my neck. I'd been so excited about my costume, but that's all it was. A costume. Something a little kid would wear on Halloween.

Kris was still smirking, but he said, "Don't worry about it. *Everybody* thinks capes look cool. But they never think about the risks. I could help you with the gloves."

"Really?" Kris hadn't talked to me in school all week. He'd kept his head down in Language Arts, leaving me to deal with Trevor on my own. Which thankfully wasn't *so* bad now that he had something to focus on other than terrible poultry puns. Trevor honestly seemed interested in the RLSH, and he knew a *lot* about superheroes. And superpets, which I'll admit, had made me laugh out loud. I couldn't imagine Superman carrying around a supermonkey named

Beppo, but Trevor swore that was a real thing. He hadn't joked about chickens once. I kind of wanted to ask Kris why he'd abandoned me, but I was afraid to bring up Language Arts. What if he asked what I was doing my how-to project on? That was *not* a conversation I wanted to have.

"No problem," Kris said. "If we cut off the hands, you can still keep the cool red armbands, but have your fingers free for maximum dexterity."

"Won't that look weird?"

"We'll make it look good. I like how you used your peacock eye," he added, nodding toward my belt. "Nice touch."

Kris led me to his bedroom, which was a complete disaster area. The air smelled like a mix of glue and stinky socks. There were Legos, clothes, and comic books all over the floor, and his desk was an explosion of model-airplane parts. One whole wall was covered in photos of people of all ages, mostly Indian, posing in big and small groups for the camera. There had to be a hundred photos. At least.

"Who are all those people?" I asked.

"Family." Kris grabbed a pair of scissors off the desk and handed me a plastic bin crammed with rolls of colorful duct tape. "Which one do you like?"

I chose a shiny black tape with yellow stars.

"*All* those people are your family?" There had to be

fifty times more people in his family than mine. And if you only counted the family I had in Maine, then a hundred times.

Kris nodded. "When I was little, we lived in Chicago and got to see them a lot, but they send us pictures wherever we are so we don't feel so far away."

Kris had lived in Chicago? That was practically Wisconsin. I wondered if he missed his family, but then I thought of all the people who'd shown up to help the Anands move to Ocean Avenue. It was like they'd built a new family. Or at least added on.

"Who's that?" I asked, pointing to a picture that didn't look like a family photo. It was a headshot, like from a celebrity, and it was signed. "He looks like you."

The guy in the picture was a muscled superhero who had Kris's thick black hair and a black mask cut into jagged edges, just like Wrecking Ball's. The word *KRRISH!!!!* was printed in big comic-book lettering near the signature at the bottom of the photo.

Kris laughed. "Thanks! I never knew I was so buff!"

If I'd been drinking root beer, I'd have done a spit take for sure. "I mean, he has your mask! And your name. Sort of."

Kris chopped the hands off my supergloves. "He's a

superhero from these old Indian movies. My auntie Priya's in love with him. She sends me Krrish stuff all the time, so I tried to make my mask look like his."

"It does," I said. "It looks cool."

"These are going to look cool, too," Kris said. He showed me how to fold the starry tape carefully around the cut edges of my gloves to make them look like red arm sleeves that *purposely* didn't have hands attached.

By the time we finished, Silver Sparrow had arrived with a sewing kit and some black fabric. Crystal Warrior was with him, but she disappeared into the back bedroom with Ekta and Willow.

"Where's the choking hazard?" Silver Sparrow was wearing his gimmick, but he took off his helmet and shook his head. Hard. A spray of sweat flew off his hair and spattered us. Kris and I yelled and ducked for cover.

"Sorry," Sparrow said. "I just finished my workout and then we were on our way to the wharf."

He had curly dark brown hair like Crystal Warrior, and without the silver bird beak, I could definitely see they were siblings. They had slightly different skin tones, but the same intense-but-kind brown eyes. People used to say Wally and I had the same nose, which, for some reason, we both thought was hilarious.

I handed over the rainbow cape and watched as Sparrow removed the drawstring and sewed a square magnet into one of the cape's corners. He was quick. In about sixty seconds flat, he'd tied off the string and moved on to the second corner.

"Are you training for football or something?" I asked. "You work out a lot."

"Nah. I want to bulk up so I can help my uncle. Here, hold still."

Silver Sparrow came at me with a needle.

"Wait a minute!" I said.

"Don't worry," he said. "I saw this on the RLSH forum. I won't stab you, but I've got to be fast 'cause Papa Wheelie's waiting in the van."

"He's good at this stuff," Kris said. "I'd trust him."

"Fine," I said, and held perfectly still while he used the black fabric to sew two more magnets, one on each shoulder of my dress.

When I put the cape and the gloves back on, I felt a thousand times better. The red arms of the gloves reached almost to the short sleeves of my black dress, and now the wrists were lined with starry black cuffs. With the cape secured magnetically to my shoulders instead of tied around my neck with a string, my Spectrum gimmick looked even cooler than it had before.

Ekta, Willow, and Crystal Warrior emerged from the back room and clapped and cheered at the improvements. Willow's gimmick had gotten better, too. Instead of the heavy leather coat, she wore a slick black vest and a black clip-on tie over the white collared shirt. The dress pants and pointy shoes had been replaced with dark leggings and black sneakers. With her eye mask, fedora, and fingerless leather gloves, she looked fierce and unbeatable.

We did the pencil test again and I managed it in four seconds. When Kris grabbed at my cape, it came right off, no choking involved. Sparrow gave me a high five, and even Ekta gave a nod of approval.

"You should come to the wharf." Silver Sparrow put his helmet back on. "We were heading down to do a quick patrol. Want to?"

"Um . . . *can* we?" I asked. Partly to Willow and partly to the Reality Shifters.

Crystal Warrior and Ekta looked at each other for a while like they were having a telepathic conversation. I let out my breath and forgot to inhale.

Then Ekta shrugged and Crystal Warrior shot me a smile that sent tingles down my arms. My whole body felt warm. Like she actually had laser eyes and was using them to fill me with strength and superpowered energy. I took a breath. Even my lungs felt stronger.

"*Spectrum . . . Miles . . .*" Crystal Warrior said our new names slowly and seriously like we were getting knighted. "Welcome to the Reality Shifters."

I tightened the laces on my superboots and adjusted my duct-taped cuffs. I put my hands on my hips in the best superhero stance I could manage. In my Spectrum gimmick, with Aunt Willow and a league of superheroes at my side, I was ready.

"Let's go change the world!"

THE WHARF

Papa Wheelie gave each of us a fist bump when we piled into the van.

"Hey! The new recruits! Right on!"

At first, I was disappointed we weren't going back to City Center. I still had the bus pass Derek had asked me to give to Pearl's mom, and since they hadn't used it, I was hoping to give it back. I didn't want him to think I'd stolen his bus pass. Besides, he might need it.

But Wrecking Ball explained that the Reality Shifters had a schedule. City Center Square and the Commercial District were part of the regular Saturday rounds. Impromptu "pickup" patrols were usually down at the wharf.

"There's always something to do down there," Wrecking Ball said. "Trash pickup, graffiti removal—you know, the kind that's not art. Plus, Papa Wheelie can't come to City Center, so we'd have to split up."

"He can't? Why not?"

Silver Sparrow shot me a funny look. "Cobblestones," he said. Like the answer was obvious.

I didn't get it.

Silver Sparrow shook his beak at me. It was sort of a relief to have him back in his helmet. There was something about him that seemed more at ease. Like he was born to be a bird.

"Wheelie's one of the toughest guys I know," Kris said. "But cobblestones are his kryptonite. Especially in City Center 'cause they're all old and mismatched. If you hit a spot where one of them's missing . . ."

"*Kkkkhhh!*" Sparrow made a crashing motion with his hands.

Right. I'd tripped on cobblestones before, but I'd never thought about trying to navigate them in a wheelchair.

"Shouldn't they do something about that?" I asked.

"If it could be done, Wheelie'd make it happen," Kris said. "He's the whole reason Port City has accessible buses."

"Really? Didn't they always have lifts?" I'd just assumed buses were *invented* with wheelchair lifts.

Papa Wheelie had been talking with Ocean and Crystal

Warrior, but clearly he'd also been listening because he leaned his head in our direction.

"No way, Little Rainbow," he said. "And it wasn't just me. A whole team of us protested for *years* to make that happen. Before any of you all were born." He put his fists in the air, flexing his arm muscles like a prizefighter, and chanted, "We will ride! We will ride!"

"That's so cool." Miles shot Papa Wheelie a starstruck grin.

It *was* cool. Superhero cool.

We left the minivan in a parking garage and started by strolling up the main pier where the ferry terminal is. Port City has a working waterfront, which means that all day there are boats coming in and out of the harbor. Ferries. Fishing boats. Cruise ships. Container ships. Even though we'd lived in Port City for almost nine months, I'd only been to the wharf twice. Once for a field trip, and once when my parents brought me to look for seals. When we first moved to Maine, we thought we were going to do stuff like that all the time. New stuff. Stuff that didn't remind us of Wally. But even the seals in the bay made us think about how much Wally liked to play in the lake. And *that* made us think about how he didn't get to do it anymore. Eventually, we quit doing the new stuff. Sometimes, it felt like we quit doing everything.

The afternoon sun sparkled on the water like stars. I kept my eye out for a seal. Or a black cormorant drying its wings. Ocean carried a pack filled with bottles of water in case we came across anyone who looked like they needed it, and Papa Wheelie had a garbage bag attached to the back of his wheelchair in case we came across any trash. But otherwise, we didn't have anything particular to do.

Honestly, it felt strange. On Saturday, we'd had a goal. Tasks that needed to be done. Today, it felt like we were just wandering around. In costumes. People stared while Ocean and Crystal Warrior handed out business cards and did the usual spiel. *Hope for the hopeless. Help for the helpless. Making Port City a better place.*

I tried to focus on shining a light, but on *what*? I couldn't help feeling a little embarrassed. Crystal's publicity speech about the "hopeless" and "helpless" hadn't felt right when we were giving out blankets, but it made even less sense now.

"There's some trash," Wrecking Ball said, and rushed ahead to pick up a take-out container that had missed a trash can.

We crossed over to another pier and made our way back to the street.

"Can I get a selfie with you guys?" a woman asked, and we posed, flexing our muscles for the camera.

Wrecking Ball and Silver Sparrow did a jiu-jitsu demonstration for a couple of kids eating ice cream at a picnic table. Then we took more selfies.

I was starting to feel silly. The new cuffs on my armbands were looking less Hollywood and more kindergarten by the minute.

Crystal Warrior caught my eye and moved next to me. She had her hair in tiny braids that swayed as we walked.

"How's Spectrum?" she asked.

I thought about saying *fine*, but Crystal Warrior always looked like she knew what you were thinking anyway.

"It doesn't seem like we're *doing* much," I admitted.

"It's all right." She linked her arm through the crook of my elbow. "Sometimes, just showing up and hanging out with your team is enough."

Your team. I didn't hate the sound of it.

My aunt joined us and linked her arm through my other elbow. "Be ready, Spectrum," she said. "Adventure is all around you."

Which is spooky when you think about it, because only a few minutes later, we might as well have been living out an adventure movie. Or a dream.

We were heading back to the parking garage when we heard the scream. Half a block away, I saw a lady throw her hands in the air and crane her neck in every direction, looking for someone or something she'd lost. But I couldn't see what she was looking for. There were a few other people milling around, but no one else seemed to notice anything unusual. In fact, everyone was minding their own business so much that I thought maybe I'd imagined it and the scream never happened at all.

"*That kid in the man bun*," Papa Wheelie said, and pushed his wheels a little faster. "I'll get behind him. You all hold the line."

The "kid" he was talking about was a man in his twenties, and I didn't get why Papa Wheelie was bothering with him. He wasn't doing anything. Only walking. Listening to his headphones. Checking his phone. Just like everyone else.

But as the man got closer, Ocean had us all stand elbow to elbow in a tight line, so our team took up the whole sidewalk. A wall of Real-Life Superheroes. That's when I saw it. A white purse tucked under the guy's arm. Not like he was carrying all his stuff in it. Like he was hiding it. He had it shoved under the side of his flannel shirt, pinned in by his elbow, so nobody would notice.

"He stole that lady's purse?" I asked.

The "kid" looked up from his phone and I'm pretty sure the last thing he was expecting to see was a line of superheroes blocking his way. He looked shocked. Then annoyed. Then worried. Without a word, he turned around to walk the other way. Where, of course, Papa Wheelie was waiting for him.

Papa Wheelie grabbed the guy's wrist and said something quiet. Ocean motioned for us to close in and I saw the purse drop to the ground. The woman who had screamed came running toward us, yelling, "That's mine! That purse is mine!"

The man swore and tried to free his arm. He even kicked Papa Wheelie's leg, which made me scream, but Silver Sparrow jumped in to help and Crystal Warrior grabbed my hand.

"Circle up!" she yelled.

Wrecking Ball took my other hand, and quick as an actual superhero, Crystal Warrior pulled us all into a circle around Papa Wheelie, Silver Sparrow, and the thief. Ocean blew on her whistle and to tell the truth, I was too stunned to be happy or excited or scared. I only knew two things. I had to stand my ground. And this guy—this criminal—wasn't going anywhere.

NABBING THIEVES

A policeman heard Ocean's whistle and jogged across the street.

"Hey!" he yelled. "What are you all doing to that man? Step away! Now!"

Silver Sparrow tugged Wrecking Ball's arm, and the two of them took several steps back, keeping their hands obviously *out* of their pockets. I locked eyes with Miles, remembering what Sparrow had told me about his dad's warning. Was the policeman going to think *we* were the bad guys? There was one horrible moment of confusion while Ekta, Papa Wheelie, and the woman whose purse had been stolen talked sense into the policeman, and we all relaxed when he finally took out a pair of handcuffs to apprehend the thief.

The thief *we'd* caught!

While the policeman got out paperwork and grumbled about "interfering" and "making his job harder," a crowd formed, and once everyone figured out what was happening, they started to applaud and cheer. For us. The Reality Shifters. Because we'd done it. Caught. A. Thief. I couldn't believe it.

Wrecking Ball danced around from foot to foot, all hopped up with energy, and did weird chest-bumps with Silver Sparrow. Miles gave me a bear hug that practically squeezed my guts out, and then Crystal Warrior threw her arms around my aunt *and* me, squeezing us both even more.

Papa Wheelie and Ocean finished talking to the policeman and then we posed for more selfies with the purse lady and the bystanders. One boy even asked for our autographs. I guess that's what happens when you're a superhero.

At one point, out of the corner of my eye, I thought I caught a glimpse of Jade's purple-tinted hair. I was so hyped up that my first instinct was to wave my hand and yell, "Hey! Jade! I'm a superhero! Bet you didn't see *that* coming!" but luckily, I remembered to keep it cool. Stay undercover. The girl disappeared anyway, and it was probably all my imagination.

By the time things calmed down and the police had

everything they needed, it was almost six o'clock. I didn't know how we were going to get home without Dad seeing us in our gimmicks. Willow didn't seem worried, though, and when Ocean invited us over for dinner and a "stuffing party" we agreed, without even asking what that meant.

It took awhile to walk the remaining block to the parking garage, partly because we were celebrating, and partly because we'd taken a side street, and the sidewalk had a high curb. In order to cross the road, you needed to take a step down. Which, of course, Papa Wheelie couldn't do.

We paused at the intersection and Wheelie took a can of spray paint out of a pocket in his wheelchair. He handed it to Wrecking Ball.

"Want to do the honors?" he asked.

Wrecking Ball grinned, shook the can, and sprayed the words CUT ME!!! in giant red letters on the corner of the sidewalk.

"*Cut me*? What's that supposed to mean?" I asked as Wrecking Ball capped the spray can and admired his work. "I thought you said the Reality Shifters *clean up* graffiti?"

"When it's covering up something people need to see, like stop signs and stuff, then, yeah," he said. "But this is a public service. We *want* people to notice."

"Another way of shining a light?" I asked.

"You're catching on." Papa Wheelie winked at me, then put his hands firmly on his wheels and tilted his chair back until the front caster wheels lifted off the ground.

"Watch out!" I yelled. I couldn't help it. It was so startling to see him balance on his back tires, but Wheelie laughed.

"You've never seen anyone pop a wheelie before? How do you think I got my superhero name?"

With his casters still in the air, Papa Wheelie turned his chair so he was facing the street, then hopped his back tires off the curb and onto the road.

"How'd you like that?" He spun his chair around a couple times, then set his casters down and reached up to give me a high five.

"Show off!" Crystal Warrior said, but she videoed the whole thing, and after all four of her uncle's wheels were safely on the pavement, she took a photo of Kris's lettering, too.

"We post these videos and photos online," Crystal said, and shot my aunt a wicked grin. "Then, after we get a bunch of comments, I send the links to City Council."

"Seriously?" Miles asked. "Do they listen to you?"

Papa Wheelie chuckled. "You'd better believe they do. The second that video goes viral, they'll be out here with a crew, cutting that curb."

"They should have done it *already*." Ocean looked angry about it. "We live in the twenty-first century and most of Port City's sidewalks *still* aren't accessible. It's criminal."

Crystal Warrior gave her a kind smile. "That's why we're here, right?"

Miles reached out and squeezed my hand as we crossed the street, and all my earlier feelings of doubt and embarrassment disappeared. I knew exactly what she was thinking. I was thinking the same thing.

Public service. Nabbing thieves.

It felt pretty great. Being in a heroes club.

COSTUME CHANGE

As we drove back to One Ocean Avenue, the sun was starting to go down, filling up the sky with cozy yellow-pink light. In between houses, I could see the mirror of the sunset on the water. Oranges and pinks mixing with green and blue-gray. I pushed my mask onto the top of my head and watched the reflection like drops of oil paint floating in a puddle. Swirls of rainbow colors, mixing and not mixing. Standing out and blending in.

Willow sat in the way-back with me and Kris, and texted Dad the minute we pulled out of the parking garage:

Upstairs neighbors invited me & Z to dinner.

Want 2 come?

"What are you doing?" I asked. I thought she wanted to keep the whole superhero thing a secret.

"Don't worry," she said. "He won't come. This way he'll feel included. He'll be less likely to be annoyed that we aren't home."

She was right. There was no way Dad was going to come to dinner with strangers.

He texted right back:

I'm good. Have fun!

"But what are we going to do when he sees us in our gimmicks?" I asked.

"He won't," Willow said.

"What if he looks out the window? Right when we're going upstairs?"

"I'll sneak you two up the back way," Kris said.

I stared at him. "The fire escape?" That rickety old ladder was nowhere near Mom's safety standards.

"It's fun."

"But what about after dinner? When we come home? I don't have a change of clothes. He'll see us then."

"ZZ, quit stressing," Willow said. "We'll put your cape, our masks, and all the other stuff in my backpack. It'll look like we're wearing normal clothes."

"I'm wearing a *dress*," I said. "That's not normal clothes."

I didn't think they were listening, but Ekta and Crystal Warrior joked from the front seat.

"Welcome to the world of the RLSH!"

"Clandestine costume changes . . . what a bear!"

"Bet you wish you had a phone booth right about now!" Papa Wheelie chuckled. They were *not* taking this seriously.

"Trust me," Willow said. "Your dad is not going to notice. If Jen was home, that would be a different story. But we'll be back before her shift's over. You can relax, Z. I promise they won't see your gimmick."

It wasn't the costume I was worried about. It was the questions. I knew Mom and Dad would want to know a lot more about the RLSH than I had answers for. I barely knew anything about these people, but we were riding around in cars with them, talking to strangers on the street, fighting crime. You didn't have to be a rocket scientist to know Mom and Dad weren't going to be thrilled about that. Or to know who they would blame if *anything* went wrong.

Willow had taken off her mask and she had her fedora tilted sideways on her head. She was grinning and joking with the others about secret identities and the logistics of quick costume changes.

"Could you imagine trying to change out of spandex in a booth like that?" she asked. "You couldn't move. Your knees would bang into the glass."

"Do phone booths still exist?" Sparrow asked. "I've never seen one in real life."

"They've got to," Willow said. "Where else would Clark Kent change into his Superman suit?"

"A Starbucks bathroom?"

Willow threw back her head and laughed. The melody of it unwound some of the worries that were tightening my chest. I leaned against her arm, and she reached for my hand. Like she used to do when we were on the dock in Wisconsin, looking at the stars. Snuggled up in a sleeping bag, three deep: Willow, Wally, and me. Me leaning against Willow's arm. Willow holding my hand on one side, Wally's on the other.

I closed my eyes quickly because sometimes it sneaks up on you. You can be going along having a perfectly amazing day making costumes and going on wharf patrol and then someone takes your hand and out of the blue your throat starts to burn because you can't help thinking about stars and brothers and how one-third of your sleeping bag is empty. When it shouldn't be. And you can't help knowing that if he were here, that missing third would be *so* on board with joining your team of Real-Life Superheroes. That he'd go nuts coming up with a gimmick of his own. And you know exactly how he'd laugh his head off talking about changing his underwear in a phone booth. If he could. But he can't. And you can't escape the nagging thought of the canoe. That tippy, tied-up canoe. And your open book, floating down to the bottom of the lake.

"ZZ?" I felt Willow's hand on my head. "We're here."

And then you pull your mask down over your eyes and blink a few times real quick so the canoe and the underwater book disappear and you follow your aunt around to the back of the house where your heart pounds a mile a minute because you are putting hand over hand on metal rungs and trying not to think about falling. Climbing. Up a wall. Like a superhero.

Wally would have died.

I mean.

He would have loved this. So. Much.

STUFFING PARTY

It turns out that a stuffing party is what the Reality Shifters do on most Friday nights to get ready for their Saturday mission. Last week, they'd set up an assembly line and stuffed sandwiches. This week, we stuffed tortillas with a mix of brown rice, peas, and lentils spiced with garam masala, then rolled them in foil and stacked them in a box in the fridge. By the time we were done, the entire apartment smelled like an Indian restaurant and my stomach was making sounds like a thunderstorm.

"It's like a mix between a burrito and a samosa," Kris said. "A burrosa. Mom's specialty."

"It's nice of you to make something vegetarian for people who don't eat meat," I said, and Ekta laughed like I'd told a funny joke. "What?"

"I'd put meat in if we could afford it," Ekta said. "You think this all comes from a food fairy?"

I blushed, because I hadn't really thought about the fact that someone had to buy the stuff we were giving away. I set down the bottle of water I'd been about to open and got a glass of tap water instead. Kris, though, grabbed a burrosa for each of us and pulled me toward the living room where Silver Sparrow sat on the couch in khaki pants and a white polo shirt, already halfway through his third burrosa.

"Are you going somewhere after this?" I asked. "You look fancy."

Sparrow's mouth was too full to answer, but he made a goofy face and popped the collar of his shirt.

"Harper goes to St. Mark's," Kris explained. "He wears the school uniform to show off."

Sparrow, aka Harper, choked on his burrosa. "It's what I had in my backpack. Don't listen to him, Zinnia." He threw a lentil at Kris. "Cool shirt, though."

Kris looked down at his T-shirt, which had an image of the superhero Krrish in his jagged black eye mask and black leather gimmick. The actor looked extra-tough with his slicked-back hair and muscled chest.

"Zin thinks he looks just like me," Kris teased, shooting me a wicked grin.

It felt weird to see all the superheroes hanging around in their normal clothes joking and using their regular names. Papa Wheelie's real-life name was Joe. He'd taken off his gloves and mask and changed into a black T-shirt in the minivan before Harper carried him up the stairs to the apartment, then ran back down to bring up the wheelchair. Crystal Warrior, aka Emilia, had washed off all her face paint in Ekta's bathroom. I barely recognized any of them without their gimmicks.

"Mom checked out Wheelie," Kris said to Harper as we sat on the floor and unwrapped our burrosas on the coffee table. "He's got a bruise on his shin from the kick. No broken skin. She said to keep an eye on his toes, but he's fine."

Harper rolled his eyes. "I keep *telling* him not to wear those sandals. He won't listen."

Kris caught me looking confused.

"Wheelie's paraplegic," he said. "He can't feel any part of his lower body, like if his toes are getting scraped up on the pavement. He must have nicked them when we were on patrol."

"Maybe when he was getting off that curb," Kris said.

"Is that . . . a big deal?" I asked.

"Only if he gets an infection," Harper said. "Ekta's our fixer, so we're good."

"Fixer?"

"If anybody gets hurt," Kris said. "Superheroes always have a fixer. Mom's a nurse, so she's ours."

Ekta was a nurse? I don't know why it surprised me. Maybe because the nurses who'd worked with Wally were sweet and cheerful and Ekta was so . . . intense.

Harper got up to get another burrosa and Kris stuffed the rest of his in his mouth before asking, "Did you see that girl from our class at the wharf? Jade?"

His mouth was full, rice and lentils mashing up his words, but I still heard every syllable. My eyes went wide.

"Was that really her? Do you think she recognized us?"

"Nah. For one, we were wearing masks. For two, it's the benefit of being invisible at school. No one recognizes us. Even without the gimmick."

I wasn't sure. Kris had said the RLSH were invisible, too, but people definitely noticed us. I know he meant it in a different way, but still.

"Hey Zin." Kris lowered his eyes and finished chewing before he said the next thing. "I'm sorry I didn't pair up with you in Language Arts."

"It's fine," I said. Even though it wasn't. I was surprised he even brought it up.

"It's not fine," he said, surprising me again. "It was a jerk move. But you were talking so loud and I got nervous that people would find out. About all this."

He nodded toward the team. Willow was in the kitchen telling a story, waving her hands exaggeratedly in the air. Joe threw back his head and laughed along with Ekta and Emilia. Harper wagged his eyebrows at us and snuck three more burrosas while Ekta wasn't looking.

"Why would it matter?" I asked. "You said not all RLSH keep their identities secret. And what about the publicity?"

Kris rolled his eyes. "It's different at school. Trust me, it's better to stay invisible. I won't give up your identity if you won't give up mine. Okay?"

"Okay." I tried not to think about the subject of my how-to project.

"Anyway," Kris said, "you got to be on a team with your friend, so it all worked out."

My mouth hung open. After that nice speech, he was going to *joke* about it?

"What?" Kris put on an innocent look.

"Real funny," I said. *Honestly. Not. Funny.*

"Seriously. What's funny?"

"I got to work on a project with my *friend*?"

Kris tilted his head to the side. "You hang out all the time. You have lunch together every day."

"Because he won't leave me alone."

"I saw you guys laughing in class today. You looked like you were having fun."

I paused. It was true that Trevor had been *not* mean and even kind of funny since we started working on the superhero project. He'd dropped the poultry jokes and had moved on to impressions and weird stories about Beppo and other superpets like Comet the superhorse and Ace the bat-hound.

"That doesn't mean we're friends," I said.

Kris gave me a funny look. "I'm pretty sure *he* thinks you are. He gave you that feather. And you put it on your costume."

What?

"We're not friends!" I said it a little too loudly. The adults stopped talking, and Willow looked my way. I didn't care. Either Kris was messing with me, which I didn't like. At all. Or he was terrible at seeing the obvious. How could he not know that Trevor Pryor was the absolute worst part of my school day? That the "tail feather" was only one in a long string of mean jokes designed to make sure no one in school thought of me without thinking "Chicken Girl." And it was *Kris's* fault that I had to spend the last period of the day with my nemesis.

"What are you talking about?" Harper asked, flopping back on the couch and offering us each a burrosa.

"There's a kid at school bothering Zin," Kris said. "I guess."

"What? Who?" Willow sat down next to Harper. "Is it the same kid who made the chicken joke you told me about? I thought that was a onetime thing."

My face burned. "It's fine," I said.

But everyone from the kitchen moved toward the living room. Emilia sat cross-legged on the floor next to me. Papa Wheelie rolled up behind her.

"What are you going to do about it?" Wheelie asked. He looked genuinely concerned.

I stared at the floor, but in my heart I scorched Kris with my laser eyes. I didn't want to talk about it with *him*, let alone with four other people I barely knew. I'd hardly even talked to Aunt Willow about it.

"Nothing," I said.

All the Reality Shifters started talking at once.

"You can't do nothing."

"He'll keep at it."

"Don't let him think it's okay."

"Have you told any teachers?"

"What's he doing that's bothering you, Z?"

I kept my eyes glued to the floor, but I knew Willow and the whole team were looking straight at me. I could feel their eyes boring into my skull. I wished I had actual powers of invisibility so I could vaporize myself. But when Emilia reached out a hand and touched my arm, I looked up. She and all the other Reality Shifters were circled around me, just like we'd circled up around Papa Wheelie and the thief at the wharf. Like they wanted me to know we were a team. And they had my back.

"That stinks, Zinnia," Emilia said. "You want to tell us about it?"

I didn't expect it to happen, but my mouth opened and the whole story spewed out. The spilled chicken soup on my first day at Oceanside. The endless poultry jokes. The constant embarrassment in front of the other kids. The name-calling and the way Trevor stuck to me like Velcro. Having every single sixth-grade class together. The tail feather. I told them everything I could think of, and as I was talking, I realized that except for the one time I'd told Aunt Willow that some boy made a chicken joke about me, I hadn't said any of it out loud before. It didn't exactly feel *good*, but I felt lighter. Like I'd been carrying something heavy, and a group of superheroes had come and taken it out of my arms.

"Have you ever told Trevor how that makes you feel?" Harper asked mid-bite.

"He *knows* how it makes me feel," I mumbled.

"Does he?" Ekta asked.

"I guess I'm not sure," I said. It seemed impossible, but maybe Trevor *didn't* know he was bothering me. Or maybe he didn't know how *much*. "Mostly I ignore him."

"And how's that been working out?" Emilia asked. She wasn't teasing me. Her voice was kind and gentle and the group nodded like everyone knew the answer.

There was a beat of silence before Joe said, "Ignoring things doesn't make them go away, kid. It's not easy, but if you want things to get better, you've got to speak up."

I thought about the CUT ME! graffiti on the curb and the years Joe had lobbied for accessible buses. If anyone knew about speaking up, it was him.

"How?" I asked.

"Sometimes you have to tell people how you want to be treated," Ekta said. "And if he doesn't get it, then you might have to tell someone else. A teacher. Kris can help you. Or we all can, if it comes down to it."

There were lots of nods and murmurs of "yes" and "you got it" and "absolutely, kid."

Even Kris, who wanted to be invisible at school, said, "Sure, Zin. I'll help."

I almost lost it right there. All their kindness made my heart crumble. I could feel it breaking off in pieces inside my chest. Before I fell apart completely, I forced myself to pull it together. I straightened up and made myself remember what it felt like to have my mask and my rainbow cape on. To be standing in a circle with your team. Strong. Invincible.

Joe had a point. If I wanted things to get better, ignoring the problem was not an option.

"Okay," I said. "I'll talk to him."

The Reality Shifters erupted into a full-on cheer. Then Ekta put on some old Motown music and Emilia started dancing with Joe. Aunt Willow took my hand, pulled me to standing, and danced me around, too.

My face was still on fire, but it was a good fire. The kind that happens when you're warm and full of burrosas and one superhero or another is passing around chocolate chip cookies and tomorrow is Saturday, which means you get to go on another mission. In your rainbow gimmick. To bring help to the helpless and hope to the hopeless. It was the kind of fire that happens when you don't feel either of those things. Helpless or hopeless. At all.

"I've been wondering about that," I said, accidentally speaking my thought out loud. We'd finished dancing and I was sitting on the floor next to Emilia, shoveling in my fifth chocolate chip cookie and feeling more than a little sleepy. Harper was snoring on the couch.

"About what?"

"I don't know. The people we gave blankets and food to. They didn't *seem* hopeless and helpless. I mean, not most of them. I guess Pearl's mom was a little bit helpless but only because her foot was hurt. Honestly . . . she seemed pretty strong."

"You think?" I hadn't meant to say anything, but Emilia looked seriously interested.

"Well, she took her kids out of whatever bad situation she was in," I said. "Even if it meant they might have to sleep on the street. That was brave. And she wouldn't have done it if she didn't hope things could be better, right? I guess . . . *hopeless* and *helpless* don't seem like the right words."

"Hm." Emilia looked thoughtful. "I'll think about that, Zinnia. Thanks."

Before we left, Emilia gave us a plate of cookies to bring to Mom and Dad. Ekta gave Willow instructions to meet up at noon. And Kris ran into his messy room and came back with a bright red flashlight.

"It's good to have a flashlight for safety," he said. "And it matches your gimmick. You can hook it onto your belt."

"Thanks," I said.

"I'm sorry I had it wrong about Trevor. But I'm glad I know now."

"Thanks," I said again.

"If it helps," he said. "I could still join your group. In Language Arts. I'm sure Mr. Iftin wouldn't mind."

I froze. I couldn't explain to Kris that I'd told Trevor about Real-Life Superheroes. Even though I hadn't spilled anything specific about Ekta or Kris or the Reality Shifters, I knew it would feel like a betrayal. Especially after tonight.

"I . . . I don't—"

"Come on, Z." Willow tugged at my sleeve and pulled me into the hall. "We've got to get downstairs before Hawk Eye gets home. See you tomorrow . . . team!"

SOCKS

"So how was it?" Dad asked in the morning. He'd been asleep in front of the TV when we got home, and now he was rushing around trying to get his recording equipment ready while the rest of us ate breakfast. "Are the upstairs neighbors nice?"

"*Super*nice," I said, grinning at Willow over my pancakes.

Mom gave me a sly sideways smile.

"They *must* be supernice," she said. "Your dad said you wore a dress to dinner."

"What?" I swiveled my head toward Dad. "I thought you were asleep when we got home!"

"*Mostly* asleep," Dad said. "Has anyone seen my yellow notebook? I've got to be in Duckport by noon. A Girl Scout troop is awarding a medal of honor to the border collie who saved their lives from a rabid skunk. I wouldn't want to be late."

His sarcasm made Willow grin. "Hey, not all heroes wear capes," she teased, and nudged my foot under the table while Dad rolled his eyes.

Mom ignored them both. "So?" She eyed me. "Tell me about this boy. What's his name?"

"What boy?"

"The one you wore a dress for."

Willow practically spit up her coffee. My fork clattered on my plate.

"No! *Mom!*"

Mom shot me a knowing smile. "Come on, Zinnia. It's okay. It was bound to happen sooner or later. Is he nice? What's he into?"

I covered my face with my hands and groaned. Willow shook with laughter while Mom launched into a story about her first boyfriend, Tim, and how he invited her to a dance or a movie or something. I didn't hear the details exactly. I was trying to block out the sound of her voice before my ears started bleeding.

"My first crush was Cynthia Brown," Dad said, pulling on his jacket. "Now, *she* was a Girl Scout. I loved it when she showed off her badges. Oh, *Cynthia!*"

"Ew. I'm not hungry anymore," I said. I pushed away my plate and glared at Aunt Willow, who was laughing so hard she was wiping tears from her eyes.

"Okay, okay," Mom said. "I'll stop. I just think it's nice. Of course, I wish you had asked me first. I should have talked to his mom before you went up there for dinner."

"It's *not* why I wore—"

"Don't worry, I'm leaving it alone. I've got to get to work, too." Mom stood up and put her dishes in the sink. "Let's go out for dumplings tonight, okay? We've *clearly* got a lot to talk about." She winked at me.

As much as I loved dumplings, I was not going to dignify her wink with a response.

"I told you they'd notice the dress," I said after Mom and Dad were finally out of the house.

Willow giggled. "It's actually the perfect cover. Now we've got an excuse for hanging out with Ekta and Kris."

"The perfect cover? It's embarrassing!"

"I know!" Willow was enjoying this a little *too* much. "But what's a little embarrassment in the service of saving the world?"

I threw a slice of bacon at her.

The worst part was that the second I got into the minivan, I started blushing and I couldn't stop. *Not* because I had a crush on Kris. I didn't. But just because my parents *thought* I did, I could barely look at him. It wasn't fair.

"Ready to rock another mission?" Wrecking Ball held out his fist as I made my way toward the back seat. I bumped it awkwardly and avoided his gaze.

"Everything okay?" he asked.

"I think I need a different costume," I mumbled.

"*Gimmick*," he said. "And no way. It's perfect. Don't you guys think Spectrum's gimmick is good?"

"I could add a rainbow border to the dress if you want," Sparrow offered.

I couldn't even answer.

We drove to the City Hall parking lot, and this time, I felt like I knew the drill. We hydrated, ate protein bars, and slathered ourselves with sunscreen, even though it was a cloudy September day. Crystal Warrior handed around backpacks filled with bottles of water and the burrosas we'd made, then passed us each a plastic grocery bag stuffed with value-packs of new white tube socks. The back of the van was full of them.

"What happened to the rest of the blankets?" I asked.

"I dropped them off with a couple of the local shelters," she said. "They're overfull right now with waiting lists, so they were glad to have some extra bedding. Today's mission is socks." She looked superexcited about it. "I had some bonus babysitting gigs this month, so I bought the nice, thick ones in bulk!"

"Socks?"

"Trust me. Clean, dry socks can change somebody's world."

Ocean checked her watch. "Let's stick with the same groups we had last time. Check in at noon."

It started sprinkling about three minutes after we got to City Center, and I'd only given out a couple of burrosas before the rain started to come down for real. I assumed we'd turn around and head back to the parking lot. But Ocean had a pocket in her backpack that was filled with thin plastic rain ponchos.

"I've got a few spares," she said. "If you see someone who needs one."

I definitely felt less like a superhero with a plastic poncho over my head. I'd never seen Black Panther or Spider-Man wearing rain gear. Miles wasn't thrilled about it. But still. We stuck together and handed out as many socks and burrosas as we could. When we spotted Mary in a doorway, covered with the wool blanket we'd dropped off last week, this time we knew to leave the water, burrosas, and socks on the ground and walk away without saying a word.

Some people in the square were sleeping, or pretending to sleep. Most of them had the blankets we'd handed out, though I also saw a few blankets shoved into corners or left in doorways. An old guy named Pete recognized us from last week and asked me if I played any instruments.

"I wish," I said, and Pete ate his burrosa while he told us all about how he played piano as a kid and wished he'd never quit.

"I could play 'The Entertainer' at lightning speed," he said, and at one point, he got so excited about the old song that he let out a loud swear word. I flinched, and Miles gave a nervous laugh and Pete felt so bad about it he kept saying "sorry, sorry, forgot you were kids—" until I interrupted him to say, "I've never heard 'The Entertainer,'" and my aunt took out her phone and looked it up so we all could listen.

"You could play that?" I asked. "It sounds superhard."

"That's what I'm sayin'!" Pete grinned.

There were two teenagers, Kaylee and Rae, in the stairwell where Pearl, Johanna, and the baby had been. They had a puppy with floppy brown ears and they asked for an extra burrosa so they could share some with the dog.

"What's his name?" I asked, handing over the burrosas and two packages of socks.

"*Her* name," Kaylee said, "is Greta. Hey, do you have any toothpaste? Or tampons?"

I shook my head, but Miles rummaged around in her bag and handed over three tampons. "Sorry I don't have more," she said. "I didn't even think of that."

"Yeah," Rae said. "Most people don't."

We stayed and played with Greta for a little while before heading back out on patrol.

"How do you have a puppy when you don't have a house?" I asked Miles when the girls were out of hearing distance.

My aunt shrugged. "Dogs are good for defense if you're on your own," she said. "And Greta probably makes them happy, don't you think?"

She *was* a cute pup.

Miles and I had been keeping an eye out for Derek because I had his bus pass in the pocket of my dress. He wasn't at Dad's building, and I hadn't seen him in any of the doorways or under the overhangs. Maybe he didn't live out on the street. I'd only assumed that because he asked for a sandwich and was standing in a stairwell with his bag. He'd certainly looked a lot more pulled together than most of the people we'd seen in the square. His clothes were clean and he seemed less tired, more cheerful. I wondered what I should do with the bus pass if we didn't see him, but then I spotted a guy with an olive duffel bag coming out of Starbucks.

"Hey! Rainbow Brite! I wondered if I'd see you again!"

GREAT DAY

Derek looked more tired than when we'd seen him before. A lot more tired. He had a bit of black beard stubble around the scar on his chin, and his eyes were bloodshot, but his smile was the same. It lit up his face and made me grin.

"I'm Spectrum now," I said.

"Nice! See? That's what I'm talking about. Simple. Elegant. None of this Panther-lasser stuff."

"She's decided to stick with Ocean," I said.

"Good," Derek said. "That's better. What are *you*?"

He nodded toward my aunt and she reached a hand out from her rain poncho to tip her fedora at him.

"Miles," she said.

"Whatever floats your boat." It was still raining, but only a little. Derek glanced around the square. "Did you see anybody over there? That doorway looks dry." He hoisted his duffel bag onto his shoulder and motioned with his other hand toward a boarded-up falafel shop that had recently gone out of business. Before we could answer, he started walking toward it, taking long strides. I almost had to jog to keep up with him.

"Do you guys have any food today?" he asked. He was still smiling but his lips were tight. Like it wasn't exactly easy to make the smile happen.

"Yeah. Burrosas. They're like a samosa in a burrito disguise."

Derek chuckled half-heartedly at my joke. He dropped his bag in the doorway and sat down on top of it. I watched as he leaned into the side of the building like he needed something to hold him up. He rubbed his hand over his head and almost didn't notice that Miles was handing him a burrosa.

"You want a water?" she asked.

"Thanks."

"We've got socks, too."

I nudged Miles. Derek wasn't like the others. He'd just come out of Starbucks. "He doesn't need socks," I whispered.

"Hey. Rainbow. I'll take 'em," Derek said. His hands

were busy shoving the burrosa into his mouth, so Miles set a package of socks next to the water bottle on the ground.

"It's Spectrum," I said.

Derek's eyes got a little more focused and he laughed. "Right. Sorry. I forgot. Good name. Seriously."

I fumbled under my poncho and pulled the bus pass he'd given me out of my pocket. I set it on top of the socks.

"We didn't need it after all," I said. "So I thought you might want it back."

I didn't know if it had anything to do with the bus pass, but Derek stopped trying to smile. Some burrosa rice spilled onto his jeans.

"Derek. Are you okay?" My aunt stepped closer and put her hand on his shoulder. She looked worried. We'd only met this guy twice, but I felt the same way. Like he was our friend. Which was probably silly, but that didn't change the way it felt.

Derek stared at the bus pass. Then he took a giant bite of his burrosa. "It's all good," he said. "Some bum luck with medical bills, but I'm like a cat. I always land on my feet. If you don't mind leaving an extra water . . ."

"Sure." I knew all about medical bills. Mom and Dad had been stressed out about Wally's all the time, and in the end, Grandma and Grandpa stepped in and helped us out. I remember Dad was so relieved, he cried.

I handed Derek another water from my backpack and looked at my aunt. I wasn't sure why, but I didn't want to leave him in the doorway, all alone.

"I walked over there the other day." He tapped the spot on the bus pass where he'd written the words *Safe Harbor Women's Shelter, 52 Scarlet, route 1, 2nd stop.*

"The place where Pearl and her mom and the baby went?" I asked. "Are they your friends?"

Derek shook his head. "Never saw 'em before. But . . . I didn't know if she had anyone to check up on her, you know?"

"Isn't that a long walk?" Miles asked. "Johanna said it's on the other side of town."

"Yeah, it killed some time. What else have I got to do?" He looked like he was perking up. Getting ready to crack a joke or two. "The little girl said if I saw the rainbow super-girl, I should tell her she made up her mind."

"The rainbow supergirl?" I laughed.

"Yup. She says to tell you she's going to be a superhero princess. Whatever that's supposed to mean."

"Were they okay?" Miles asked.

"They were still there, so I think that's good. It's a safe place to be."

"Do you . . ." I wasn't sure if we were friends enough to ask, but I plowed ahead anyway. "Do *you* need a safe place to be?"

Derek smiled and shrugged a shoulder. "I'm on a waiting list right now," he said. "For affordable housing. But honestly, these guys need it more." He nodded to the piano player. "Pete's been on the list for three years."

"Three *years*? What about the others?" I looked around the square, and Derek studied me, like he wasn't sure how much I really wanted to know.

"Okay, good question," he said finally. "Mary needs a different kind of help. Doctors and stuff. Those girls with the puppy show up now and then. They were in foster care, but they aged out. They need more than a place to stay—to finish high school, for one. That guy, Gerry." He nodded toward the sunburned man we'd seen last week who was still holding the GO HOME! sign. "I don't know what hurt him, but he's plain mean, so I don't ask."

Miles frowned. "It sounds really complicated," she said. "Like, more than a burrosa can fix."

"That's for sure," Derek said. "The burrosa's not nothing, though." He finished his off and Miles handed over another. "Thanks," he said. Then, "Want to hear something bonkers?"

We nodded.

"I got a job interview today. They want me to come in on Monday."

"Really? That's good," I said. "Right?"

"Yep, and it's even farther away than Safe Harbor. Six miles farther. I had no idea how I was going to get there." He shook his head and winked at me. "But now I think I'll take the bus."

I grinned.

Derek pointed toward the sky. Where the sun was starting to poke through the clouds.

"Did you make that happen, too?" he asked. "You might be newbies. But tell Ocean I said you're doing all right."

When we met back up with the rest of the Reality Shifters, everyone was exhausted, cold, and wet, but all of the burrosas and most of the socks had been given away. We hadn't saved the planet, but because of our patrol, some of the people on it were warmer, less hungry, less invisible. I didn't even care that I was soggy and my teeth were chattering. It was worth it. It was a great day.

"Good work, team," Emilia said as we piled into the van. Even *she* looked tired. She pushed a few wet braids out of her face as she started the engine and pulled out of the parking lot.

"Did your group get any action?" Ekta asked from the front seat.

"Nope," Harper said. He sounded disappointed. "Not like yesterday."

Aunt Willow shook water off her fedora. She'd seemed tired and quiet since we'd left Derek, but the mention of the purse thief perked her up. "Now *that* was action," she said. "I can't believe we actually nabbed a thief!"

"Best. Patrol. Ever," Kris said.

"I hope we get some publicity out of it," Ekta said.

Kris leaned forward in his seat. "Don't you wish stuff like that happened more often?" he asked. "We're superheroes. We should be fighting crime." He muttered the next part quietly so only Harper and I could hear it. "The eXtreme eXamples don't waste their time with *socks*."

I thought about it. We *had* been pretty fierce—standing in that circle, trapping the thief. I'd felt powerful, part of something big and important. But I knew what we'd done today was important, too. Even if it was less like a movie. And a lot colder.

"Yesterday was a great day," Harper said.

"*Super*great," my aunt agreed.

Joe hadn't said anything since Harper strapped his chair into the van. I figured he was tired like the rest of us, but he'd started tapping his fingers on the metal rim of his tire. Turned out, he was mad.

"A great day?" Joe's voice was quiet but it had an edge to it. Like it could get a lot louder, real quick. "A *great* day will be the day we go out and no one needs us. When no one's getting hurt or having anything taken from them. NO one's hungry. NO one's cold. *That's* the kind of 'great' day I want to have!"

"Simmer down, Joe," Ekta said. "We didn't mean anything."

"It was exciting, that's all they're saying." Emilia looked at her uncle through the rearview mirror and tried to get him to smile. "Even you have to admit that days like today are kind of a slog."

Joe scowled. "Think about it. What you call 'action' means something terrible is happening to somebody. It's not exciting, and it's not something to be happy about. It's definitely not something to *wish* for."

The minivan was quiet for a minute, and then Willow spoke up. "I get that," she said, "but I think Kris is right, too. Catching that thief was really doing something. Maybe we should focus on that."

"Meaning?" Joe asked. I found myself leaning forward in my seat.

"We stopped a crime," Willow said. "That guy's getting

punished and the woman got her purse back. It was a problem, and we solved it. It's over. Right?"

Kris nodded. "Exactly. Justice!"

"Ka-*kaw!*" Harper said.

"And?" Joe eyed my aunt.

She fiddled with her fedora. "Those people today ... they're all still out there with no place to sleep. You know? One sandwich a week doesn't solve anything. They need more than dry socks. The problem is too big."

Emilia looked at Willow through the rearview mirror. "That's why *we* show up," she said, starting in with her movie voice. "When systems are overworked and underfunded, when apathy is in the *air* around us, what the world really *needs* is superheroes like us to—"

"But we aren't really," Willow said quietly. "We're not superheroes. So ... we might as well volunteer at a soup kitchen."

I stared at her. The mood in the van had gotten tense. I knew Aunt Willow had a point. Mary. Pete. Kaylee and Rae. Sure, maybe they were less hungry because of us, and they had clean, dry socks on their feet. But their lives were essentially the same as they were yesterday. It's not like we swooped in with superpowers and shifted reality for them.

Derek, though. I'd brought his bus pass back, and now he

could get to his job interview. *That* could be life-changing. And Pearl, who was going to be a superhero princess for Halloween—she was in a safe place. Wasn't helping her and Johanna get a taxi a *little* heroic? I wasn't sure what to think.

Joe cleared his throat. "She's right about one thing. We're not *heroes*," he said. "That's not what it's about. But we're out here doing what we can. You all worked hard today, so I'm going to do you a favor, and I'm going to forget all that nonsense you just said."

We drove the rest of the way to One Ocean Avenue in silence. No one even mentioned the faint rainbow hovering in the sky. No matter what direction we turned, it was still there in the clouds like it was following us home.

DUMPLINGS

Willow and I barely made it out of our gimmicks before Mom came home. She walked in the door seconds after I'd changed into jeans and a sweatshirt. My fingers were icicles and my hair was still damp from the rain. Dry clothes never felt so good.

"Did you *just* take showers?" she asked, hawk-eyeing our wet hair. "Don't tell me you stayed in your pajamas all day."

"You're home early," I said.

"Fatuma agreed to cover for me so I could have a little extra time to hang out with my sister. I told her you were visiting and I wanted us to have a fun day."

Mom smiled at Aunt Willow, but I felt like she'd put extra pressure on the word *visiting*. I didn't love the sound of it.

I was afraid she was going to push the issue and bring up college, but instead, she made a pot of hot tea and pulled out a thousand-piece kitten puzzle she'd borrowed from the café's game shelf. By the time Dad got home, we'd put together all the edge pieces, and I was almost done with the entire body of an adorable orange-furred kitty.

Still, something felt forced about Mom's "fun" day. I could tell there was a catch. She was holding it in, and she waited until we got to our favorite dumpling restaurant to let it out.

"Mom and Dad called today." Mom reached for a soup dumpling, clamped it between her chopsticks, and dropped it on her plate, letting it cool while her statement sunk in.

I looked at Willow, but she didn't seem to hear the same warning bells in Mom's voice that I did.

"Oh, yeah? How are they doing? Is it getting cold there?"

Mom glanced at Dad and he gave her a slight nod. I stopped chewing. Something was up.

"They wanted to know how your visit for Zinnia's birthday went. They said they haven't heard from you since you got back to Madison."

Willow blew on a dumpling and shoved the whole thing in her mouth.

"They said they didn't want to *bother* you because you

must be busy," Mom said. "With school. And your research fellowship."

Willow nodded and waved her hand in front of her mouth like the steam was too much to handle.

"*Hot*" was the only thing she said.

"Grandma and Grandpa think you're at school?" I asked. "Didn't you tell them you're *staying* here?"

Willow locked eyes with me. I tried to read her mind. Probably she kept it a secret because her parents wouldn't understand. They'd worry. It made sense. I knew what it was like to have parents who worried.

"Not yet," she said.

"But you are. Staying. Right?"

"She can't just quit school, Zinnia," Dad said.

"Yes she can," I said. "If she wants to. You *want* to, right?"

Willow nodded. But she shifted her eyes to look at the table instead of at me.

"What about tuition?" Dad asked. "It's almost October. I don't know if you can get a refund this late in the game. That's a lot of money, Willow."

"They're *my* loans," she said. "I'll pay them off. Don't worry about it."

"I'm worried about your *degree*," Mom said. "What are you going to do without a college degree?"

Willow had been looking stressed. Guilty. A little sad. But now she was mad.

"*You* don't have a degree," she said, pointing her chopsticks at Mom. "You dropped out of nursing school when you got pregnant with Z."

"You were in nursing school?" I asked.

Dad caught my eye and shook his head at me like he was asking a favor. *Let it go. Stay out of it.*

"That was different," Mom said.

"Not really." Willow shrugged. "Your priorities shifted. So have mine."

"Your *priorities* have shifted?" Mom was trying to keep her voice calm, but it wasn't working very well.

"I want to do something that matters. I want to make a difference in the world."

"Can't you make a difference after you get your degree?" Dad asked. He said it in a nice, jokey voice. Like that was going to help anything.

Mom didn't even try to joke. She took it straight to the next level. "You can't keep disappearing every time things get hard, Willow. Life gets hard sometimes. It's called being an adult."

Willow threw her napkin down on her plate and pushed back her chair. "I'm going to the bathroom," she said.

I watched her leave the table, and even though Dad had given me his pleading eyes, I couldn't stay out of it. They were being completely unfair. It was Willow's life. She should be able to do what she wanted. Especially when she wanted to stay with *us*. With *me*.

"At least she's *doing* something," I said. "At least she's *trying* to change her life."

"Zinnia, you don't understand."

"I do, too. Isn't that why we moved to Maine? To start fresh? Change our lives?" I chewed my lip, and when they didn't answer, I added something more. Almost under my breath. Almost a mumble. "How'd *that* work out?"

Mom and Dad froze. My hands had started shaking and I set my chopsticks down on the table. The last thing I wanted to do was keep talking about it, but I wanted them to let Willow stay. So. Badly.

"I'll tell you how it worked out," I said, but I kept my eyes on the blue dragon design on my plate. "Not great. We moved halfway across the country and nothing changed. Nothing. Except now we're all alone."

I tried not to notice that Dad reached out to hold Mom's hand. Or that both their eyes were filling up with tears. My throat felt like it had a soup dumpling lodged halfway down, but I swallowed it and lifted my chin.

"Everything's better since Aunt Willow came," I said. "You guys think so, too." They did. I knew they did. Mom had laughed more in the last week than she had in the last year. And Dad hadn't had a single one of his phone-scrolling days. "Why would you want to send her away?"

Even after Willow came back from the bathroom, my parents didn't say anything. No one did. We sat in silence while the waitress brought over one last plate of dumplings that nobody touched.

PHOTOS

Dad was the first one to break.

He put on a fake cheerful voice and made a joke about how we must have scared off the waitress with our family drama and now we were never going to get the check.

"Get comfortable," he said. "We could be here all night."

No one laughed, so he pulled out his phone. I could see how my night was going to go. Mom and Willow giving each other the silent treatment, and Dad, tuned out, scrolling through photos of Wally.

Instead, Dad made one more attempt to break the ice.

"Here's another interesting story," he said, tapping his phone. As if we'd been laughing and chatting about fascinating items in the news. "Dawood's doing a piece about a guy who got caught stealing a purse down at the wharf."

Mom could barely pretend to be interested, but Willow and I sat up a little straighter in our chairs. Dad knew about the purse thief?

"Check out the photo he sent me. The thief was stopped by . . . wait for it . . . *superheroes!*"

I knew Dad was trying to lighten the mood, but this wasn't helping. I bit my lip and shot Willow a panicked look. He had a photo of the superheroes down at the wharf. My parents already wanted Willow to go home. If they found out we'd been driving around talking to strangers and fighting crime with a random bunch of real-life super-heroes, they'd probably kick her out right now for being a bad influence.

"I'm glad I didn't get *that* assignment," Dad said, making a face.

"Why?" Willow broke her silence. "You'd rather cover the Girl Scouts and their dog hero?"

Dad chuckled, and even though Willow was obviously annoyed, he looked hopeful. Like maybe if he kept talking about superheroes, we could shove the previous conversation under the table and pretend it never happened.

"Um, let's see," he said. "A bunch of ego-driven comic-book nuts who think they can fight crime? Yeah, it's worse."

I stiffened, and Willow scowled.

"How do *you* know what they're like?" I asked.

"I've seen these guys around," Dad said. "They do some nice things, but they're only in it for the attention. Check it out."

He held out his phone, and I bit my lip as we all leaned in to look. Even in my cape and mask, there was no way Mom was going to miss Grandma's first-day dress or my rainbow tights. I hadn't thought about that when I was creating my gimmick. Being recognized.

"Wait, is that . . . ?" Mom took the phone from Dad.

I held my breath as she zoomed in on the superheroes circled up, holding hands at the wharf. I exhaled as she pointed to Silver Sparrow.

"He hangs out by the Goodwill," she said. "I don't know about *superhero* but he's *super*weird. *Super*sketchy."

"He's not sketch—" I started, but Willow nudged my foot under the table.

Miraculously, the photo only focused on Crystal Warrior, Silver Sparrow, Ocean, and Papa Wheelie. Miles was cut off at the shoulder, and the rest of our circle was off-camera completely. But it didn't make me relax. I couldn't help remembering the selfies we'd taken with all those random people on the street, and the family at the Ice Cream Shack. How thorough was Dawood's research going to be? I'd met him a few times at Dad's office. What if he'd recognized me at the wharf? What if he already knew it was me?

"Isn't it bizarre?" Dad asked.

"It's sort of . . . cool?" I tried to look noncommittal. Like a random observer, just offering another perspective. Not like it *mattered* to me.

"It's reckless is what it is," Mom said. Dad's new topic wasn't improving her mood.

"Reckless?" Willow and I blurted it at the same time. So much for noncommittal.

"How?" I asked.

Mom rolled her eyes. "Regular people shouldn't try to fight crime, Zinnia. It's dangerous and it's not smart. The police train for stuff like that. They know how to handle criminals."

"But the police weren't *doing* any—"

Willow kicked me under the table again and Mom held the phone closer. I didn't like her examining the picture so closely. Only one of Miles's superhero arms was visible, but Mom had superpowers of her own.

"Are there more?" She swiped her finger across the phone to scroll through the photos and I sucked in my breath. I hadn't even thought about there being *more*.

But the next photo was of the falafel place where Derek had been earlier today. He hadn't looked so good. I hoped he'd found someplace to sleep. Indoors.

Mom scrolled through a couple close-up shots of the building's brick wall. She gave Dad a look. "Walls, huh?"

"That's Alice's story," Dad said. "She's probably going to win a prize for it. Keep going."

Mom scrolled through several photos of the brick walls at Dinah's Café, Donut Depot, and Boni's Bakery. Dad said, "This summer, there was a spree of laptop robberies in every one of those shops. People would be sitting studying or working and suddenly, their laptops got snatched right out of their hands by a group of thieves."

"Fatuma and I heard about that," Mom said. "We're lucky it never happened at the Powerhouse."

"Alice thinks the robberies are all connected," Dad said.

"Really? How?" Willow looked interested. I shot her a grateful look. She was doing a good job. Distracting Mom from the superheroes.

"See that spray paint?" Dad zoomed in on a brick wall. The letter was small, so at first you hardly noticed it. But if you looked closely, you could see someone had sprayed a miniature red X in bright red paint. "Alice thinks that tag is the common link," Dad said. "It's still a theory right now, but she thinks someone is marking shops that will be easy to hit."

"Like a signal?" Willow asked.

"That's terrible," Mom said.

It *was* terrible, but I couldn't help but be glad that those robberies got the focus off the Reality Shifters.

"Alice is a great reporter." Dad sighed. "One of these days, I'm going to ask to switch to *real* news . . ."

I tried to hold in my eye roll, but I must have had *some* look on my face, because Dad's voice faded out. His smile faded, too. He stared at me. Like suddenly, everything I'd said ten minutes ago had finally sunk in.

"Hm," he said quietly.

I wasn't wrong, but he looked so sad, I wished I hadn't said anything about moving to Maine or loneliness. If Wally were here, this was exactly when he would have done something hilarious. Some weird elephant noise or made-up joke that made zero sense. He would have done whatever it took to make our whole table laugh so hard that somebody—usually me—spit up their drink and had to ask the waitress for extra napkins so we could clean up.

But Wally wasn't here. And I was never the one who could think of something funny to do. When the waitress finally came with our check, I asked her for more napkins. It was an inside joke. Inside my own head. So it made sense that no one laughed.

I felt a little better anyway.

PLATE TECTONICS

At home, Willow put on her penguin pajamas and turned on the reading light. I climbed into my sleeping bag on the floor. I told myself we could all go to sleep and start over in the morning. It could all be fine.

Mom knocked on the door to say good night. Which could have been quick and pleasant. Willow could have closed her book and said *Good night, thanks for dinner*, and Mom could have said *Sweet dreams*. We could have turned out the lights and closed our eyes and woken up to a new day. A fresh start.

Instead, Willow said, "Jen."

She patted the space on the bed next to where she was sitting, but Mom didn't come in.

"Jen, I really need your support right now."

I waited for Mom to rush to Aunt Willow's side. Pat her

back. Tell her little sister that everything was going to be all right.

She didn't. She chewed her lip and let out a breath.

"And I really needed my sister, Willow," Mom said. "I *needed* you there."

Mom's voice was a whisper, but it was strong enough to make Willow's eyes close. It felt like the whole house went silent. Even the usual nighttime elephant thumps from upstairs were missing. I lay still as stone, and Mom rested her head against the doorframe, both of us waiting for Willow to say something. But her eyes stayed closed. That's when I knew I'd been dreaming. That it was definitely *not* going to work out. Willow was going to leave. My life was going to have another hole in it. My room was going to feel even emptier than it had before.

Mom stepped back out into the hall and closed the door. The second the latch clicked into place, Willow reached over and turned off the lamp. Another *click*. I heard her book hit the floor. The blankets rustled. She sighed. It all sounded louder than it should have, like the creaks and groans of a tectonic shift, new cracks forming and settling into place before the quiet seeped in again.

A sound cut through the darkness.

My voice.

"Why'd you disappear, Willow? When Wally got sick?"

I hadn't forgotten it. I'd just let myself not think about it. How Willow had vanished the whole summer before Wally died. Not literally. She lived one mile away at my grandparents' house. She'd just finished high school and hadn't even started college yet, so it's not like she had homework or anything else to do. But she stopped coming over. Stopped telling us stories. She'd say she was coming. "I promise, ZZ," she'd say on the phone. "I can't wait to see you!" But my grandparents would show up without her, and there was always some excuse. Willow had to practice. She had to work. She was camping with her friends.

Later that summer, after Wally's surgery, when we knew the cancer had spread to more parts of his brain, when we knew the radiation probably wasn't going to help, Willow promised more. We'd do a whole weekend sleepover together. She'd bring her constellation book. She was practicing a song on guitar to play for Wally. And me.

But none of that ever happened. The last time she saw my brother was four whole months before he died. It was early June, and Dad had just put in the dock. We'd celebrated Willow's graduation the week before, and she came over with her graduation cap. Wally wore it all through dinner. He had a hard time keeping it balanced on his bald head, but he thought it made him look "professional" and he liked that it made everyone laugh. Plus, the cap covered up the marks the doctor had drawn, like a treasure map on Wally's skull, to get ready for the surgery he was going to have in a few days. Wally hated those marks. He said they looked like tattoos and he wasn't a pirate.

After dinner and graduation cake, Willow took us down to the dock with our sleeping bag. It was freezing, but the sky was clear, and we cuddled up, looking at the Milky Way, a cloudy smear dotted with stars.

"That's the path Cygnus's friend burned in the sky, right?" Wally said. "Phaethon? When he stole the sun chariot and raced it across the sky."

Wally giggled. He loved the part about the sun chariot.

But suddenly, he choked on his giggle, turned on his side, and puked all over the dock.

"Ew! Wally!" I said. I squirmed out of the sleeping bag and grabbed a sand pail from the shore. Earlier, we'd been making sandcastles, and then writing stories in my journal about Captain Walleye's fight against the dragons that destroyed them. He'd puked then, too, but we'd gotten used to that happening sometimes. We wrote it into our story, making one of the dragons a mutant with pukepower instead of firepower. That was the best kind of adventure, Wally had said. The kind with an unexpected twist.

"We should go in," Willow said, looking worried.

"It's fine," I said. "Just move over."

Willow and Wally stood up while I dipped the pail in the lake and used the water to rinse the dock. The last of the ice on the lake had only melted a few weeks ago, and the water was freezing cold. A breeze kicked up.

"For real," Willow said. "We need to go in."

"I don't want to go in," Wally said. "I want to get back in the sleeping bag. I want to hear the story."

By then, his eye was doing that weird wiggle thing that meant the tumor in his brain was pushing up against his optic nerve. Wally called it his Magic Eye and pretended he was controlling his eyeballs with a wizard's wand.

"Wally. Magic!" I said, pointing at my own eye to let him know it was happening again.

Wally waved his fake wand in the air, but Willow scooped up the sleeping bag in a panic.

"It's okay," I said. "It's only pressure on his brain. It'll stop."

"Please," Wally said, getting mad. "Don't treat me like a baby."

"The stars are really good tonight." I pointed up at

Phaethon's Milky Way, Orion with his bow, and Cygnus the Swan. Willow only looked at the constellations the doctor had drawn on my brother's shaved head. I wished he'd worn the graduation cap outside so she wouldn't notice so much.

Wally stomped his foot, ready to throw a tantrum, and Willow shook her head.

"I can't," she said. They were the same words she used the whole rest of the summer. Even after the words *I promise*. And when summer ended, she left for college. She joined a band. They had a gig the day of Wally's funeral. My grandparents drove all the way to Madison to pick her up, but when they came back, hours before the service, Willow wasn't with them. She'd promised to come with her guitar. To play her song. The one she'd been working on. Instead, the church was silent.

"I wanted to come," Willow whispered.

In my bedroom, at One Ocean Avenue, my ceiling stars glowed in the shape of a swan. Stuck. For eternity. I could feel my pillow supporting my head, but my body felt floaty. Like I was up near the stars, too. Hovering in place in my sleeping bag.

"I couldn't take it, ZZ," my aunt whispered again.

Well, I couldn't either. None of us could. But what else were we going to do?

I felt a tightness in my throat, like my neck was being stretched. My arms lay stiff, glued to my sides. I thought of a few things to say. *It's okay, Aunt Willow. You're here now. We love you. We've always loved you. We will always love you.* But questions sprouted like feathers, covering up the words.

Will you stay?

Do you want *to stay?*

What can I do to make you want to stay?

I couldn't say any of it. My voice was frozen in my throat. So I listened to Willow's exhales, soft and steady, punctuating the silence.

Stay.

Stay.

Stay.

FROZEN

When I woke up, Willow was sitting on the floor, packing her Miles gimmick into a suitcase.

"Morning, Z," she said when she caught me looking at her. Like everything was fine. "Do you think Emilia wants these leggings back?"

I didn't answer her. My head felt heavy. What was she going to do, quit the team? Exactly like Ekta had predicted? Mom had warned me to keep my expectations low, but Aunt Willow was *supposed* to prove them both wrong. I wanted to grab the leggings from her and throw them back into her messy pile on the floor where they belonged. But I didn't. I turned on my side and pretended to go back to sleep.

I didn't feel like talking later, either. To anyone. All day, I felt weird. Like a supervillain had zapped me and stolen all my strength. If I were a real superhero, I would *do* something about it. Pull myself together. Fight back. But I didn't. At dinner, I opened my mouth to say *No thanks, I don't want any asparagus*, but then I closed it again. I didn't even care that my plate got filled with a pile of slimy green spears that I didn't want to eat.

I nodded when Dad asked if my throat hurt. Even though it was a lie and it made Mom stress out that I had strep or pneumonia. It meant they let me stay home from school for two days. I stayed in my pajamas the whole time and hawk-eyed Willow while I watched TV, worked on the kitten puzzle, and ate ramen. My aunt barely seemed to notice I was there. She spent most of her time on the computer or her phone, sighing and biting her lip. Finally, on Tuesday afternoon, she set the phone down and rubbed her eyes.

"Do you want to go for a walk, Z?" she asked.

I shook my head but pulled my blanket up, making room for her on the couch. I didn't feel like getting out of my pajamas or going outside, but I wanted her to come sit by me. Maybe if I looked extra-pitiful, she'd realize how much I needed her in Maine.

But Willow put on a sweatshirt, and said, "Okay. I'll see you later then," and I didn't even remind her that I'm not supposed to stay home alone.

She didn't come back until just before Mom's shift was done, and then I worried that she looked antsy. Bored.

On Wednesday morning, Mom took me to the clinic. The doctor told her it was possible I'd had a virus over the weekend with lingering laryngitis, but I looked healthy now. So Mom drove me to school. I got there in time to sit through a video about how we should use a "growth mindset" to train the neural pathways in our brains to learn math. There was a cartoon guy in a car driving on a highway inside someone's skull.

"Each time I drive this path, it gets *wider* and *stronger!*" the cartoon driver shouted with a maniacal grin. "Let's *tryyyy* it again!"

It was so cheesy, the class went berserk, laughing and hooting, copying the cartoon voice until our math teacher had to shut off the video and tell everyone to settle down. I tried not to think about it, but Wally would have loved the idea of race-car drivers in his brain. It was impossible not to imagine him playing out crash scenes every time he couldn't walk straight.

By lunchtime, the Moose Island sixth graders had a new catchphrase. It seemed like everyone in the cafeteria was quoting the mini-race-car driver and imitating his mad-scientist grin. Out of the corner of my eye, I saw Jade doing the grin and waving her hand in my direction. I knew better this time. I set my lunch tray on an open table and didn't bother looking behind me to see who she was waving at.

"Let's *tryyyy* it again!" Trevor yelled in my ear, and plopped his tray down two inches from mine. I flinched and leaned over, trying to hide my food from his view. I knew he was going to have a field day with the chicken nuggets on my tray. Instead, he pulled a crumpled piece of paper out of his front pocket.

"Where have you been?" he asked. "Are you okay? Were you sick? I've been carrying this around for days. Check it out . . ."

I put a soggy french fry in my mouth and thought about what Kris had said about Trevor thinking we were friends. Could that possibly be true? Then why was he always thinking up ways to torture me? I didn't even want to guess what was on the piece of paper he'd been waiting to share. Once, he'd brought in an anatomically correct diagram of the inside of a chicken that he must have spent hours, maybe days, drawing. All the organs and biological parts were labeled and color-coded. At the top, it read, AN ANATOMICAL STUDY OF Z. H. Our teacher was so impressed with it that she put it up on the classroom wall. I always wondered if she knew that the Z. H. stood for me: Zinnia Helinski.

Trevor smoothed out the paper and I stopped chewing. It was a printout of a webpage called the RLSH Database.

"I found this over the weekend," Trevor said. "There are more than a *thousand* entries. This page only shows the Real-Life Superheroes listed in Southern Maine. Look! We've got two teams right here in Port City. How cool is that?"

My eyes scanned the page. It was a list of real-life superheroes and their "vital statistics." There were definitely some names I knew, but plenty of others I didn't.

Superhero: PAPA WHEELIE

Location: Port City, Maine

Team Affiliation: Reality Shifters (former affiliation: eXtreme eXamples)

Identity: public

Alter Ego: Joe Robinson

Age: 51

Colors: blue and orange

Skills: military training, extreme upper-arm strength, disability advocacy

Status: active

Superhero: SCAR

Location: Port City, Maine

Team Affiliation: eXtreme eXamples
Identity: secret
Alter Ego: unknown
Age: 22
Colors: black and gold
Skills: martial arts, superstealth, crime-fighting
Status: active

How did they get all this information? They'd listed every member of the Reality Shifters, plus five members of the eXtreme eXamples, the Reality Shifters' frenemy team. The ones who only did secret night patrol and crime-fighting.

"Did you see that one?" Trevor pounded his finger on the page near a ketchup smear.

I swallowed. I did see it.

Superhero: WRECKING BALL
Team Affiliation: Reality Shifters
Identity: secret
Alter Ego: unknown
Age: 11
Colors: blue and black
Skills: jiu-jitsu, parkour, reconnaissance
Status: active

"That kid's *our* age," Trevor said. He dangled a french fry in his fingers and dripped more ketchup on the page. "Do you think they go to our school? What if they're in our class? They could be somebody we know. Or not. I mean, maybe they go to Southport or St. Mark's."

I tried to look uninterested. Tried to keep everything I knew about Wrecking Ball from showing up on my face.

"Here's what I'm thinking." Trevor pointed another fry at the page. "Some of these people don't have secret identities. We could track them down. Ask questions. Get some clues."

This was getting out of hand. I shook my head. Hard.

"Don't you want to know who Wrecking Ball is? The kid?" Trevor looked frustrated. Like he expected me to be a whole lot more excited about this than I was. "Why aren't you *saying* anything?"

"Shhh," I said, and looked around for Kris.

"Right," Trevor said, and leaned in closer. Like we were hatching a conspiracy together. "We should keep it on the down-low. Until we know who it is. We're like superhero detectives now. Right? Zinnia? Seriously, are you okay?"

I definitely was not okay. I stared at my chicken nuggets and prayed for the bell to ring. Or for Trevor to miraculously move on. Let it go. Forget about the database. Forget about the RLSH. The lunch lady had put a juice box on my tray even though I didn't want it. I hate apple juice. Couldn't she tell that was why I was shaking my head?

Someone behind us yelled, "Let's *tryyyy* it again!" and everyone in the lunchroom laughed. Except me. Trevor Pryor was the *king* of trying it again. And again. And again. He'd stuck to chicken jokes for more than a semester. There was no chance he was going to let go of an eleven-year-old Real-Life Superhero named Wrecking Ball. He'd track down Papa Wheelie. Crystal Warrior. It wouldn't take long for him to discover Wrecking Ball's alter ego. And then what?

"Hey, Zin, mind if I sit here?"

Kris put his tray down next to mine and I tried to swallow my panic. What was he doing? Kris *always* sat by himself at lunch. It was part of his invisibility plan. Which meant he was doing this for me. Out of solidarity. So I wouldn't have to sit with Trevor alone.

"What are you guys . . . oh . . ."

Kris's voice trailed off the moment he saw the printout on the table. He obviously knew exactly what it was. I could feel his eyes on me, but I couldn't look at him. My head hurt. All I could think about was how Trevor Pryor was like a pit bull. Once he got his teeth into you, he *never* let go. Just clamped down harder and shook you around for the fun of it. He'd done it to me, and if I didn't do something about it, he was going to do it to Kris.

At the stuffing party, I'd promised the Reality Shifters I'd stand up to Trevor. With all those superheroes around me, it had seemed like it was going to be easy. I'd felt strong. Confident. Supported. But in the Oceanside Middle School lunchroom, I wasn't any of those things.

Papa Wheelie's voice echoed in my head.

If you want things to get better, you've got to speak up.

Well, what if I couldn't?

"Hey, are you going to drink this?" Trevor picked up my juice box. I'd been trying not to look at it. Even the *thought* of apple juice makes me queasy. Trevor unwrapped the tiny white straw and popped it through the foil hole, squirting juice all over my arms. I wouldn't doubt if he'd plotted the whole thing.

I picked up my tray and bolted.

WORDS

I hid in the bathroom most of the afternoon.

Each time the bell rang, the door opened and a group of girls came in to check their hair and put on lip gloss. Each time, I acted like I'd just walked into the bathroom, too, and locked myself into a stall until they left.

My brain was on a constant worry loop. Worried that Trevor would figure out Wrecking Ball's secret identity. That Kris wouldn't want me and Willow on his team anymore. That Willow would go back to Wisconsin. That Mom was so mad at Willow, we wouldn't even talk to her once she was gone. That we wouldn't talk to *anyone*. That Trevor Pryor would be the only one talking to me. That Trevor would figure out Wrecking Ball's secret identity. That Kris wouldn't want me and Willow on his team anymore . . . The loop kept going for two whole periods.

The door swung open again, and I rushed into a stall and waited for the flushing toilets and chitchat to fade away. If I'd counted right, there was one more period until the final bell.

"Are you taking the bus today?"

"Can I borrow your brush?"

"Oooh, I love that sweater."

"Zinnia?"

I froze. Someone stepped close to the stall I was in.

"Zinnia, that's you, right?" The person on the other side of the door laughed, and said, "Of course it is, you've got the coolest boots in school. Can I wait for you? We can walk to L.A. together."

I didn't have much choice. I flushed the toilet, even though there was nothing in it, and unlatched the stall door.

Jade stood by while I washed my already-clean hands.

"I tried to catch your attention at lunch," she said. "I mean, it's okay if you don't want to sit with us. I know you have your own friends."

What was she talking about? She almost looked nervous.

"Um, don't you have your books? The bell's going to ring any second."

That's okay, I'm not going to class. I opened my mouth to say it, but Jade leaned in and locked my arm in hers.

"Sorry to be an annoying fangirl, but . . . that was *you*,

right?" She bent her head close to mine as she led me toward the bathroom door. "Friday? At the wharf?"

I blinked at her. Kris had said we were invisible. But Jade had recognized me—even in my Spectrum gimmick.

She pulled me out into the hall.

"The Doc Martens," she said. "They're a dead giveaway. What are you? A superhero or something?"

Kids swarmed around us, jostling each other. Some were still yelling, "Let's *tryyyy* it again!" I felt a little breathless. Like the lights were too bright. Like my jaw was too tight. Like if I heard that catchphrase one more time, I was seriously going to lose it.

Jade didn't seem to notice anything unusual. She half dragged me to Mr. Iftin's class, then let go of my arm, saying, "Anji and I are going to meet for ice cream again on Friday. If you want to come this time. I mean, you're probably busy."

This time. What was that supposed to mean? A terrifying thought crossed my mind. What if the note she'd passed me in the lunch line had been meant for *me*? What if Jade tried to invite me to ice cream and all I did was throw the paper at Anji and pretend I had to pee? I felt briefly nauseous.

Someone tapped my shoulder. I was at my desk, but I didn't exactly remember sitting down. My temples were pounding. I turned my head to find Trevor sitting at the desk behind me, holding something invisible between his thumb and forefinger. I knew this was it. This was the moment I was supposed to speak up. Be brave. Tell Trevor his jokes made me uncomfortable. Ask him to stop.

"It's a feather," I heard him say. "I found it sticking out of your shirt."

No, you didn't.

"Here's another," he said. He reached toward the shoulder of my sweatshirt, pretending to pull out another invisible feather.

I don't like that.

"Jeez, how many of these do you have?"

Trevor laughed, and I saw Kris lean over in his seat. I tried not to meet his eyes. I didn't want to know how mad he was at me.

"Hey," he whispered. "You okay, Zin?"

Zin. Even after he saw Trevor's printout. Even after he knew I'd blown his cover.

No.

I'm not okay.

No.

Trevor reached toward me again and this time, he added, "Let's *tryyyy* it again!" in the same goofy cartoon voice and all of a sudden, eight whole months of clucking and puns and feathers flashed in front of my eyes. Again. And again. And again.

My face got hotter. A thousand degrees hotter.

Breath rose up in my chest. A tsunami of breath. Breath so strong it pulled me out of my chair. Pounded through my lungs. Jerked my head forward until I was leaning over Trevor Pryor. The Reality Shifters had told me I should talk to him, explain how his actions made me feel, but right now, my breath was taking over. And it was filled with rage.

"STOP IT! STOP IT RIGHT NOW!"

Words. Real words. Out-loud words.

Mr. Iftin rushed toward me. "Zinnia? Is everything okay?"

Kris was at my side, too. I could feel him touching my arm, but I shook him off. The angry breath kept flowing out of my mouth. Shoving the words past whatever it was that had swallowed my voice.

"I DON'T HAVE FEATHERS!" I shouted. "I'M NOT A CHICKEN! I DON'T *SMELL* LIKE A CHICKEN! I DON'T *CLUCK* LIKE A CHICKEN! I DON'T *WALK* LIKE A CHICKEN. I HATE CHICKENS! I HATE CHICKENS! I HATE YOU, TREVOR! I HATE YOU!"

"*Zinnia*, let's calm down." Mr. Iftin had stepped in front of Trevor, who wasn't smiling anymore. His lips had frozen into a worried frown. His eyebrows were crumpled in confusion. He looked devastated, like he was a five-year-old I'd just punched in the stomach. This wasn't how this was supposed to go.

"Zinnia—what are you—I'm—" he stammered, like my breath tsunami had stolen *his* words now.

"Anji, can you please walk Zinnia down to the office?" Mr. Iftin asked. "I'll call ahead to let them know she's coming."

My legs felt like jelly. They didn't want to hold me up anymore. My hands were shaking and sweaty. And even though the whole class was watching in silence, it seemed like I was far away, looking down at them from another planet. My worry loop had stopped, and now all my brain had left in it were two words. I wasn't exactly sure who they were for: Trevor or Kris? Mr. Iftin? Willow? Wally? The words were small, but they took up all the space I had left.

I'm sorry.

SORRY

Wally loved apple juice. It was his thing. *One* of his things. We had a whole cupboard full of juice boxes and he was allowed to have one whenever he wanted. He was always walking around with a juice box hanging out of his mouth. We found those skinny white straws everywhere around the house, even after he was gone. In the bathroom. In the carpet. There were probably twenty in the bottom of the canoe.

That was his other thing. The canoe. He always wanted to sit in it. To pretend he was steering down river rapids in an undiscovered jungle. That summer, it was what he wanted to do more than anything. Drink his apple juice and go on a safari. Discover a new species of wild alligator. Or a portal to another world.

So even though it was the last day of September and too cold for being out on the lake, Dad hadn't put the canoe away. He'd left one end tied up to the dock so that Wally could climb in whenever he wanted to go on an adventure. Only Wally wouldn't do it without me. He needed me to write them down, all the journeys we took. I filled my journal with scientific discoveries (the world's largest butterfly, flying alligators, a mysterious invisible rat) and near-death experiences (like when Captain Walleye's canoe got covered in molten lava and he stayed alive by breathing through a juice-box straw). Wally was the explorer. The adventurer. I was the historian.

It was a tsunami that tipped us over. Not just any tsunami. A tsunami of piranhas. The waves crashed over us. Silver fish flashed their fangs. The canoe filled with water and snapping teeth. It rocked side to side, drifting out to sea with the storm.

"Wally, stop!"

More piranhas attacked and Captain Walleye's canoe rocked and swayed until the boat was almost out of control. Icy water soaked through the shoes of the trusty historian. Who hadn't wanted to come on this mission in the first place.

"Knock it off, Wally. I'm not kidding. Wally!"

When we hit the water, neither of us thought to hold our breath. So we came up sputtering and choking. Shivering in our soaked jeans and soggy sweatshirts. Wally was laughing, but he was spitting up water. And other stuff, too. I didn't want to know what. His lips were blue and he looked so frail, standing there in the shallow water, shaking with cold and giggles.

"Wally!" I yelled. "It's not funny!"

"That . . . was . . . epic . . ." He could barely even get the words out. He could barely breathe he was so cold.

Suddenly, I couldn't stand to look at him. I couldn't stand to see his teeth chattering or the water dripping from his hair to his chubby cheeks. The medications he was on had made him gain weight, and his hair hadn't grown back quite right after the surgery. He looked so sick. Not like he used to look. Not like my brother at all. I couldn't tell anymore if I was trembling because of the cold or because of the fear that had been building up ever since the doctor told us he couldn't get all the cancer out. That some of it was still inside my brother and there was nothing they could do about it. I'd felt the fear growing inside me then, pushing up against my lungs, my heart. Just waiting for a tsunami of piranhas to unleash it.

"It was *not* epic!" I yelled. "It was stupid! Idiotic!" I hurled every insult I could think of, even though I didn't mean any of it. I didn't even care about getting wet. But I didn't *know* if he was going to be okay and the words kept coming and somehow I convinced myself I wasn't yelling at Wally. I was yelling at this *impostor*. This shivering stranger who'd taken over my brother's body and ruined it. Who was stealing him away from me.

I yelled and I yelled until Wally quit laughing and went inside. He looked deflated. Defeated, like my words had given him a black eye.

My journal, with all our adventures, had floated to the bottom of the lake. It was at my feet. I could have bent down. Picked it up. Dried it out. I could have saved it.

The doctor said our "adventure" had nothing to do with Wally's death. That it was only a coincidence. Only a fluke. *Only* is a small, sad word.

Here's the thing I hate the most. Adults say it all the time: Be grateful. Be grateful for the time you had. But they don't know. How you can't possibly be grateful when Wally deserved more time. Lots more time. At least enough time for me to say *I'm sorry*.

ANGER & CHOCOLATE

Mom came to pick me up. She was still in her Powerhouse apron, which meant she'd had to leave work in the middle of her shift, but she didn't look mad. Just exhausted. Like me.

I sat in a blue plastic chair while Mom and the school counselor introduced themselves. I'd visited the school counselor plenty when we lived in Wisconsin, but not once since we'd moved to Maine. I tried to listen to them talk about the weather, but it was hard to concentrate. I couldn't stop thinking about apple juice. And the stories I'd left sitting on the bottom of the lake.

I heard Mom say, "The end of September is hard. For all of us."

The counselor nodded like she understood, and I cringed, waiting for everything that comes next.

When you're a kid and your brother dies, there are a lot of adults who want to help. Teachers. Pastors. Random people your parents went to high school with. They want to give you hugs and pat your knee. Tell you he's in a better place now. Everything happens for a reason.

But they don't know. They don't know that they're sitting too close. That telling you he's in a better place makes you feel like *your* house and *your* family weren't good enough. And 100 percent of the time, when you ask them, "What reason?" they blink. Change the subject. Ask if you want more apple juice. They don't know how much you want them to *stop* touching you. Or that apple juice makes you gag. So you can't blame them. But still.

At my old school, the counselor's office felt like a hospital room and he spent most of the time looking sad for me and asking me to draw pictures of how I felt. Sometimes he dabbed at his eyes, which made me feel worse. This lady, though. She smiled. Like she was *glad* I was in her office instead of in Language Arts with Mr. Iftin. And Trevor, who I'd screamed at. She pushed a bowl of chocolates in our direction.

"Want one?" she asked.

I shook my head. Even though I did want one. Badly. But I'd just thrown a temper tantrum in the middle of class like a two-year-old. I didn't deserve chocolate.

Mom shook her head, too, even though chocolate is her favorite thing besides pizza. I wondered if she thought she didn't deserve it, either, or if she was just trying to be polite.

"I didn't mean to get so mad," I said, remembering the look on Trevor's face. The other kids had watched me like I was a monster. Rampaging out of control. Anji had walked me down to the office and I stayed as far away from her as possible so she wouldn't have to be afraid I was going to bite.

I'd expected Mom and the school counselor to look at me the same way. But they didn't. They nodded. As if screaming at your classmates made some kind of sense.

"Sometimes I get so mad, I feel like I'm going to explode," Mom said. "Like, actually. Bits and pieces. Bones and hair."

"You *do*?" Mom was so pulled together. All the time.

The school counselor said, "It's okay to feel angry, Zinnia."

I blinked at her. It didn't *feel* okay. I was pretty sure Trevor didn't think it was okay. Or Mr. Iftin. Wasn't that the whole reason we were sitting here?

"I'm serious," she said. "There are lots of things worth getting mad about. The tricky part is not letting the anger take over. Not using it to hurt other people."

I looked at Mom. She was biting her lip the way I always do.

The counselor smiled at me again. "Do you want to tell us what happened in class?"

I didn't, really. But just like the night in Kris and Ekta's apartment, when the Reality Shifters had circled up to listen, the soft, kind way she asked it made me tell her everything. The whole history from fifth-grade chicken soup to now. Mom reached out to hold my hand. And this time, the words came out a little easier.

Mom and the counselor were quiet for longer than I expected. I figured Mom was upset that I hadn't told her about any of this before. Both of them were probably trying to figure out what my punishment should be.

"Well," the counselor said finally. She didn't look so happy anymore. "Sometimes it takes getting angry to realize things need to change."

She leaned forward, like she was about to say something else, but instead, she took one of the chocolate Kisses out of her bowl and unwrapped it. "What other kinds of things make you mad?" she asked. Popped the chocolate in her mouth. Like she'd only invited us in here to chitchat.

I let go of Mom's hand. I wasn't sure how to answer. In a way, it felt strange that I wasn't getting in trouble. But the truth was, there were plenty of things that made me mad. Furious, really. I didn't want to talk about some of them, though. Like death. Especially in front of Mom.

"When people don't have enough food," I said. "Or places to sleep."

Mom looked surprised, but the counselor nodded.

"That makes me mad, too." She didn't say anything else. Just chewed on her chocolate and rolled the foil into a little ball. Somehow the words, saying them out loud, were making me feel stronger.

"If someone doesn't want to go to college," I said. "They should be able to make their own decisions."

Mom stiffened, but the counselor nodded for me to keep going. I didn't plan to. I was going to leave it at that. But then I added more.

"I hate it when people say they're going to do something and they don't," I said. "Like they say they're coming over but then they go camping with their friends. Or they don't show up to something really, really important. Just because it's hard."

My hands clenched and Mom bit her lip again. I regretted saying it. Any of it. What was wrong with me? It was like once I'd opened it, my mouth wouldn't shut up.

"That one really gets to you, doesn't it?" the counselor asked.

"I guess." I'd been upset with Mom for being mad at my aunt. But was *I* mad at Willow, too? I frowned at the chocolate bowl. Why weren't we talking about Trevor?

"We should . . . probably go home," Mom said.

I wanted to go, too. But the counselor plucked another chocolate out of the bowl and balanced it on her palm.

"Here's what I think," she said. "It's hard to be a human. Sometimes it helps to say it out loud. Ask for what you need. If you let things slide for too long, they can pile up and get really heavy."

I thought about the heaviness I'd felt all afternoon, sitting on the bathroom floor. As much as I still felt awful, I had to admit, talking had made me feel a little lighter.

"And, Zinnia." The counselor pushed her hand with the purple-foil-wrapped chocolate toward me. "It sounds like you want other people to be happy, and that's really good. But it's okay to look out for yourself, too."

I hesitated, but took the chocolate. I peeled off the foil and let the sweetness melt in my mouth.

We were almost out the door before the counselor called us back. Mom had finally realized she was still wearing her apron, and took it off, folding it in her hands and blushing.

Weirdly, the counselor was blushing, too.

"There's . . . one more thing," the counselor said. "I'm afraid this is partly my fault."

Which seemed like a stretch. I'd never even met her before.

"I'm the one who put you in all those classes with Trevor," she said. "I thought it would help him. He talks about you all the time. 'My friend Zinnia this, my friend Zinnia that.' I didn't know."

It took me a minute to process what she was saying. For the first time, my eyes focused in on the nameplate next to the chocolate bowl: MS. PRYOR. I almost choked. The school counselor was Trevor's *mom*?

"It's possible my son might not have realized he was bothering you . . ." Ms. Pryor stopped herself. "That doesn't make it okay. I'm going to talk to him."

My face burned. What was she going to say to him?

"And I'll rearrange his schedule. I think you deserve some space. I'm really sorry I didn't know the full story."

She and Mom talked a little more but I barely heard a word beyond "rearrange his schedule." I felt a weird mix of guilt and relief. Guilt because Kris had been right. Trevor thought I was his friend. Now that I'd completely crushed that illusion, I felt bad about it. I knew he didn't have anyone else. Then again, neither did I, and that was partly Trevor's fault. He never left me alone. The only almost-friend I had was Kris and maybe Silver Sparrow, and Trevor was ruining that, too.

Besides, if Trevor Pryor *wanted* me to be his friend, he

should have been nice. The fact that I wouldn't have to sit by him in class anymore made me feel a little giddy. Like I got a get-out-of-jail-free card in Monopoly. Better, even. Like I could put on my Spectrum gimmick and jog right up Memorial Hill without even breaking a sweat. Maybe I would.

I took two more chocolates from the bowl on my way out. One for me and one for Mom. She looked like she needed it.

COMET

When we pulled up to One Ocean Avenue, I could see Willow across the street at Hilltop Memorial Park. She was sitting on my bench looking out at the bay.

Mom stopped the car in front of our house, but we didn't get out. Both of us stared out the window at the back of Willow's head. She wore her Miles fedora and she slouched on the bench. My aunt has terrible posture.

"I think you're right, Zinnia," Mom said.

I turned to look at her. "About what?"

"It's her life. She can stay. If she wants to stay."

I couldn't believe it. Two hours ago, my life had fallen apart, and now miraculously, it was patching itself back together. I didn't have to go to class with Trevor anymore. Willow could stay. Aunt Willow could *stay*.

"Are you still mad at her?" I asked. "About Wally?"

"A little," Mom said. "But that's not fair either. She was just a kid. And being a human is hard."

She winked at me and I reached over the seat to hug her. It was awkward, with the armrest in the way, but Mom stretched her arms around me and kissed my head.

"I'm really sorry," she whispered. "About that boy at school. I wish I'd known."

She hugged me tighter until we knocked over the travel mug in the cup holder and spilled cold coffee all over Mom's pants.

Mom laughed. I loved the sound of it. "I should have left the apron on," she said, dabbing at the coffee with a napkin. "Speaking of which, I've got to get back to work. Go give Willow a hug for me. I'll see you after my shift, okay?"

I practically flew across the street. I felt like if I had my Spectrum cape on, I could have done it at superspeed.

"Willow! Willow!" I yelled before I'd even gotten to the other side of the crosswalk. "Mom says you can stay!"

Willow swiveled around on the bench and grinned at me.

"ZZ! You got your voice back!" She scooted over to make room for me, but I didn't want to sit. I stood in front of her, bouncing from foot to foot.

"And I don't have to have classes with Trevor anymore!"

I told her everything, but I couldn't stand still, so we walked the path while I explained about Trevor, the RLSH database, my total meltdown in Mr. Iftin's class.

"It was weird," I said. "Kind of scary. I felt like Phaethon, when he lost control of the sun chariot. Like I didn't have any power over what my body was doing."

"Has that ever happened before?" Willow asked. "Losing control like that?"

Once. I almost said it. I saw it in my mind. Wally and the tipped-over canoe. My book, with all our adventures, sitting on the bottom of the lake. But walking down to the ocean with my aunt—who could *stay*—I felt too happy to talk about any of that. With every step, the meltdown, the worry loop, all of it faded further away. It felt like Mom and I had been in Ms. Pryor's office days ago, not hours. And now, my steps felt like they were actually taking me somewhere. Moving *forward*. Toward a new start. Just like Mom and Dad had promised.

We passed by the playground and the man on the swings was kicking his feet, as usual, singing "Somewhere Over the Rainbow" at the top of his lungs.

"Zinnia." Willow laughed. Because I'd actually jumped up on a bench. Actually started singing along. "Get down from there. That's disrespectful."

She said it because of the plaques. Every bench in Memorial Park had a plaque dedicated to someone who'd died. *In loving memory of Anna, you're in my heart forever (1975–2011). John, beloved father, beloved son (1942–2019). Honest, brave, and true: Abigail, we won't forget you (1922–2008).* I kept hopping up on the benches anyway. I didn't think they'd mind. The people on the plaques. Or the people who put them there. They probably liked "Somewhere Over the Rainbow." Maybe they wanted a new start, too.

"ZZ," Willow said when we came back to my bench. *Our* bench. Where you could see the whole park laid out, and all the fun places we were going to explore.

Even though her voice was kind of gaspy from walking back up the hill, I could hear it. The I'm-sorry tone. Only it wasn't I'm sorry for something she'd already done. It was for something she was *going* to do.

"I e-mailed my professors," she said. "They said I can make up my work and finish the semester."

"Mom said you don't have to go back," I said. I thought I'd already explained it.

"Let's talk about it later," Willow said. "When I can actually breathe." It was supposed to make me laugh. Supposed to make me forget what she was trying to tell me.

"What about the Reality Shifters?" I asked. I knew Kris

probably wouldn't want me back. He'd be mad that I'd told Trevor about the RLSH, and I wouldn't blame him. Maybe I'd have to quit the team. But he couldn't ban Willow, too.

Willow crinkled her nose. "I don't know," she said. "What do you think about all that? Kind of weird, right?"

"Weird? How?" I thought Aunt Willow said she was *born* to be a Real-Life Superhero.

"Sure, the idea is great, but we haven't done anything we couldn't have done without the costumes."

"*Gimmicks*," I said. "What about that lady's purse? We caught a thief! You were excited about *that*, right?"

"That was pretty cool," she admitted. "But how do we know the police wouldn't have gotten the guy anyway?"

"What if they didn't? The police can't be everywhere."

"Honestly," Willow said, "I started to have doubts . . . and then I saw that photo your dad had. You've got to admit, we looked pretty cheesy."

"We looked pretty *great*," I said. "I mean, your gimmick could use some work . . ." I looked at the fedora on her head and stopped myself. "Besides, it's not about looking cool. It's about *shining our light* and bringing attention to the problems of—"

"Is it, though?" Willow asked. "Or is it about bringing attention to the *Reality Shifters*?"

That felt like a low blow. "I thought you wanted to make a difference."

"I do, ZZ," Willow said. "But . . . I don't even like superhero movies that much. It's maybe not the best fit for me."

I couldn't believe we were having this conversation. It was *Willow's* idea to join the superheroes in the first place. It was *Willow's* plan to make a difference in the world. Do something interesting. Stop sleepwalking through life. And we'd done it! What more did she want?

I'd thought all my anger had been used up on Trevor, but it turned out I still had some left for my aunt. I tried to inhale. Tried not to let the anger take over my breath. I remembered what the school counselor had said. About anger being a sign that something needs to change. About not using it to hurt other people. I was mad at Willow, but she was my favorite person on the planet. There had to be a way to change her mind.

"What if we had an even bigger mission?" I asked. "Something huge and important. Like, stopping another crime. Would you stay?" As if helping people who had no food and no place to sleep wasn't *already* huge and important? I wanted to yell that at her, but I took another breath and tried to think of a mission that Aunt Willow would stay for.

"Maybe. If it was an *extra*-cool mission," she said. "I don't know, Z. It's not really about that. I kind of just have to go back."

She stood up from the bench and stretched her arms. Her eyes fell on the memorial plaque she'd been leaning against. I usually tried not to look at it much, but I had it memorized. I liked the feel of it against my back. *Liam came into our life like a comet. His visit was brief, but bright enough to light the sky (2011–2017).*

"Are you *sure* you only picked this bench for the view?" she asked.

I didn't answer her, and Willow turned to look out at Wing Island. The guy on the swings had gone home with his aide, but you could almost still hear "Somewhere Over the Rainbow" drifting around in the breeze. *Someday I'll wish upon a star / And wake up where the clouds are far . . .* I didn't have a star to wish on, but I scooted over and rested my back on the plaque. The one Liam's family, whoever they were, had dedicated to him. And I didn't exactly make a wish, but I thought about it. Waking up with all those dark, heavy clouds—the ones that had piled up—disappearing behind you. Getting farther and farther away. I thought about saying things out loud. Asking for what you need. Change. New starts. Blue skies. Rainbows.

"Will you at least stay for Sunday?" I asked, shifting so I could feel the metal plaque against my shoulder blades. "It's the last day in September. Wally's Day. It would mean a lot to Mom."

And me.

"Sure, Z," Aunt Willow said. "I'll stay through Sunday. I promise."

It wasn't enough. The promise or Sunday. If I wanted more, I was going to have to make it happen. Myself.

NEW MISSION

I don't know if it had anything to do with the almost-wish I made on the bench in Hilltop Memorial Park. Or if I just *wanted* it to happen so badly that I conjured an extra-cool crime-fighting mission out of thin air. One that would make Willow remember why she wanted to be a superhero in the first place. Remind her that she *belonged* here in Port City. With the Reality Shifters. With me.

It even crossed my mind that Wally might have something to do with it. Laughing and waving his wand from somewhere up in the sky. I didn't exactly believe that. But it seemed too perfect. That I would *need* a new mission and then suddenly there it was. Like magic.

Mom had come home for dinner, but promised Fatuma she'd return to close up the café at eight as a thank-you for covering Mom's shift while we ate chocolates in the school counselor's office.

"I'll come with you," I said. Mostly because Willow wasn't doing anything but texting with her Wisconsin friends. And packing. Which she didn't need to do. Sunday was still four whole days away. I didn't like the look of my room without her piles of stuff all over the floor.

Mom and I walked the two blocks to the Powerhouse Café, and I saw it almost immediately. Even though it was dark out. Even though the red spray-painted letter was down toward the ground on the alley side of the café with a dozen other colorful words and designs. It was practically invisible, but the way the light from the streetlamp fell, it was like there was a bolt of lightning drawing my eyes straight toward a small red X. It looked exactly like the markings in the photos Dad had shown us. He said every time it showed up, a shop in the neighborhood got robbed within days.

I didn't tell Mom about the paint. For one, she would have panicked. Or maybe she wouldn't. Maybe she would have stayed calm and done nothing. But what if she called the police? Or told Dad? Dad would probably call Alice, that reporter he knew from work. And she would start investigating, looking for the scoop. I didn't want any of that to happen. This was *my* mission. Why else would I be the one to see it exactly when I needed it most?

Mom frowned when we got home and I told her I had to run upstairs to talk to Kris.

"It's late," she said. "Almost nine thirty and . . . your dad and I don't know them very well."

"Please?" I said. "I *have* to."

"Oh *really*?" She smirked, and for a moment she looked like she wanted to tease, but stopped herself and let me off easy. "Sure, honey," she said. "It was a tough day. He'll want to know you're okay."

I'd almost forgotten about school. Trevor. The RLSH database. The fact that I might be the exact last person on the planet that Kris would want to see.

I had to knock on his door anyway. I didn't have a choice.

As I stood in the hall and waited for someone to answer, I did have a small moment of doubt. A tiny, nagging voice that sounded a lot like Papa Wheelie. Reminding me *not* to wish for bad things to happen, just so we could be heroes. But that wasn't what I was doing. I wasn't wishing for anything bad. I'd seen a sign that something bad *might* happen, and I was going stop it. That was a good thing. And if it made Willow decide to stay, was it wrong to be happy about it? Excited even? I mean, we were going to save the day.

Ekta opened the door and looked surprised to see me. Which made sense. It was late on a school night. And I may have unintentionally sabotaged her son.

"Um. Hi." I felt weirdly nervous. I'd never come up with a superhero mission before. I didn't know if there was a process. Crystal Warrior seemed to be in charge of all the planning. I decided to talk fast and get it over with. "I was hoping we could have an emergency meeting. For the Reality Shifters. Maybe tomorrow? It's important. Really important."

Ekta paused. She looked confused. "I already texted Willow. She said you guys were too busy."

"Too busy for what?" I asked.

"The emergency meeting," Ekta said.

We stared at each other.

"Well?" she asked. "Are you coming in or aren't you?"

She held open the door to the apartment. The Reality Shifters were gathered in the living room. Like each and every one of them had telepathically gotten my message.

I sat on the floor next to Kris. I wanted to talk to him. To ask him if he was mad that I'd told Trevor about the RLSH. I wanted to apologize, but the meeting had already started and everyone else was talking. Kris waved at me, though, which wasn't the worst.

It took me a minute to realize the Reality Shifters

weren't meeting about the graffiti I'd seen. Instead, they were all talking about a news story. About the thief at the wharf.

"It was awful," Emilia said. "The way they spun it. We sounded like . . ."

"A joke," Ekta said. "No offense."

Apparently, someone at Dad's radio station had tracked down Crystal Warrior and Silver Sparrow to interview them for the story.

"I said I wear my star sapphire because it's tuned to the heart." Emilia looked pained, her hand on the pink stone she always wore around her neck. "I didn't say I thought I had *mind-reading* powers!"

"At least they didn't call you Crow Boy," Harper said. "I knew ka-*kaw* wasn't a good catchphrase."

"The best way to fight bad press is to get good press," Ekta said. "Change the narrative."

"But *no one* takes us seriously," Emilia said.

"What if we did something like the Pacific Crusaders did in California?" Kris offered. "Remember when all the RLSH teams got together for a group patrol? That was in the news for weeks."

Joe shook his head. "Midnight Hawk told me it took over a year to coordinate that event."

"I have a mission we could do," I said, but everyone kept talking, comparing stories about Midnight Hawk and other RLSH they'd seen in the news. Kris took the opportunity to scoot a little closer to me.

"You okay?" he asked. He looked worried, not mad. Which was a relief.

"I'm sorry," I said. "About Trevor and the database. I didn't mean to—"

"Yeah, he told me about your L.A. project."

"He did?" I braced myself.

"At lunch," Kris said. "After you . . . took off."

"I'm sorry," I said again. "I promise, I never told him anything about *you*. Or the Reality Shifters."

"I know you didn't. It's fine."

"It is?" I couldn't believe Kris was letting me off so easy. After all that talk about keeping everything secret. Maybe he was being nice because he felt sorry for me. Because of my meltdown.

"He's really into it," Kris said. Like Trevor Pryor was a fascinating research subject, not my personal tormentor. "And he knows a *ton* about comics and superheroes."

It was true. Trevor had talked my ear off about them for the past two weeks. Apparently, he memorized superheroes like some people memorize baseball stats.

"And Zin"—Kris lowered his voice—"I think he's actually really sorry."

"Maybe we should let the whole thing blow over," Emilia was saying. "Ignore it and it will go away."

There was a knock on the door and everyone hushed. When Ekta opened it, though, we all cheered.

"Miles! You made it!"

Aunt Willow barely stepped into the apartment. "Jen sent me to get Zinnia," she said. "School night and all. We can't stay, but . . . happy superheroing."

She gave an awkward wave and started to leave. She expected me to follow right behind her. So did everyone else. They waved at us both and went right back to talking.

"Wait! Aunt Willow!" I said. "I have a mission we need to do." No one was listening. I stood up and raised my voice. "My dad works for that radio station," I said.

Suddenly, everyone quieted down. Ekta narrowed her eyes, like maybe Willow and I were spies. Moles, planted to take down the RLSH with one bad radio story.

"He's a reporter," I said. "And he might help us. I know how to get a good story. A *really* good one." I glanced at Willow, who'd taken a step into the apartment. "It's an extra-cool mission. I promise."

Finally, I had their attention. Willow came into the living

room and sat down on the arm of the couch. Everyone else leaned in. Listened carefully while I explained about the Powerhouse Café and Alice's theory about the spray-painted Xs.

"What do you think we should do?" I asked. "Like, a stakeout? So we can be there to catch the thieves when they come?"

"Do you think we could get access to the roof?" Kris asked.

"Ohmuhgosh, yes," Willow said. "We could watch from up there, and eventually when they show up—"

I grinned at her. There was no way that doing research for a college class could compare to fighting crime from rooftops.

"The roof?" Ekta asked. "Even if you see something— which is unlikely—what are you going to do, jump from the top of a building? You're not Spider-Man. You'll break your leg."

"Right," Harper chimed in. "Besides, we need to be visible. I think we should keep watch in *front* of the shop. In plain sight. No one will steal anything if they see a bunch of superheroes are there."

"No way. If all we do is keep the criminals away, we'll never *catch* them," Kris said.

"I agree," Willow said. "We need to stay hidden."

"What we *need*," Joe said, "is to alert the police."

Everyone shushed as he held up his phone.

Kris looked annoyed. "Why? We can handle this."

"I'm with Uncle Joe," Emilia said. "This is serious. They need to know. Besides, this is why we left the eXtreme eXamples, right? They were always looking for trouble. I don't like it. Sorry, Zinnia."

The group started to argue. About the police. Roof patrol. Stakeout strategies. Self-defense tactics. None of it mattered to me because Willow had the old sparkle back in her eyes.

I smiled to myself. I pretty much felt like a hero already.

Until Joe dialed the number for the police station.

"*Come on*—" Kris started to complain, but Joe gave him a steely stare. Strong enough to make even the toughest superhero back down and ask the police for help.

We listened to Joe explain everything about the red Xs and the impending robbery to the dispatcher on the phone. Then he had to explain who *he* was, and why he wanted to help. We listened to him say yes, he was the same Joe Robinson who was affiliated with the Real-Life Superheroes. No. No, he wasn't with the eXtreme eXamples anymore. He explained about the red Xs again. He suggested that they call the reporter named Alice. No, he didn't know her last name. No, he'd never made any prank calls. Absolutely, this was not a threat. Then he had to explain who he was again.

When Joe got off the phone, the room was silent.

It turned out that Emilia was right. *No one* took us seriously. Not even the police.

"I still don't like it," she said to her uncle. "But I guess we can't do *nothing*."

For the rest of us, Emilia put on her serious RLSH voice and even though she wasn't in costume, you could feel the superhero radiating from her like a force field. Full of power. Urgency. Strength.

"Sometimes . . . you choose the mission," she said, emphasizing every word. "But sometimes the mission chooses *you*."

Joe pulled a notebook out of a pocket in his wheelchair. "I'll set up a surveillance schedule," he said. "But it's only Wednesday. If we're going to do full-time patrol, possibly through the whole weekend, we need more people. Anybody got a problem with that?"

He gave a meaningful nod toward Ekta and Emilia.

"Fine," Emilia said. "Invite the eXtreme eXamples."

Ekta didn't look happy. "I don't want any of their shenanigans," she said. "We need ground rules."

But Harper looked pumped. "I bet Scar can start tonight. We could swing by and ask him on our way home."

Joe nodded and scribbled something in his notebook. *Scar.* That was one of the superheroes named in the database Trevor had found.

Willow was back to her old self. Sitting up on her heels. Grinning. Laughing and chatting with everyone else. Making plans.

This was exactly how it was supposed to go.

JADE & ANJI

It was hard to sit through Math class knowing that at this very moment, the Powerhouse Café was under RLSH surveillance. By not just *one* superhero team, but *two*. Joe was going to text my aunt the schedule, with two to three superheroes on patrol at all times. I hoped nothing would happen until school was over. Even though I wasn't supposed to *hope* for anything. Last night, before Willow and I had gone downstairs, Joe had given us that lecture all over again. Ekta had joined him and kicked in an extra dose of stern. This wasn't about *us*. It wasn't exciting. Or fun. We were only doing what we needed to do to keep the city safe. It was deadly serious. And if any of us couldn't handle that, we could leave.

But it was hard not to be excited about the mission. I could barely sleep. Neither could Willow. I heard her rustling around half a dozen times in the night. And when I woke up in the morning, all the pieces of her Miles gimmick had been pulled out of her suitcase, piled up next to unpacked books and unpacked socks. It was hard not to be excited about that, too.

Aunt Willow promised to wait for me before she looked at the schedule Joe sent. Even though he said he would send it by noon. She said we'd look at it together the second I got home.

The day dragged, but at least without Trevor in my classes, I felt like I had more elbow room. Like I could spread out, take up more space. I didn't have to hunch my shoulders in homeroom. Or keep my head down during study hall. In Math, a few kids were still saying "Let's *tryyyy* it again," but without Trevor breathing down my neck, it seemed less painful. Almost funny, actually.

I didn't even see him in the hallways, so for most of the morning, I thought maybe he'd been transferred to one of the other Oceanside Middle School "islands." Pine Cone. Or Blueberry. On my way to lunch, I felt a strange pang of guilt, imagining Trevor sitting at a table by himself. It didn't make sense that *I* was the one who felt bad, but I did. I couldn't help it. He didn't have anyone else to talk to, and I knew how that felt.

But when I walked into the cafeteria, Trevor wasn't alone. Kris was sitting next to him. Smiling. Waving his hands like he was telling a hilarious story. He spotted me in the lunch line and waved me over. Like I was going to come sit with them. Even if Kris was right, and Trevor was sorry, did he actually think, after everything that had happened, that we were going to want to eat *lunch* together?

Besides, Kris always sat alone. That was his thing. If he was going to sit with anyone, he should sit with *me*. We had so much to talk about. We had a mission to plan. I wanted to know more about the eXtreme eXamples. And Scar. I bit my lip and sat down at an empty table near the door.

"Is it okay if we sit here?"

I looked up and was surprised to find Jade standing in front of me with her lunch tray. She didn't wait for an answer. She plopped right down at my table and Anji sat next to her, unzipping a baby-blue lunch box.

"Um, you were really fierce yesterday," Anji said. I couldn't tell if she meant fierce in a good way or fierce like the rabid skunk who'd chased all those Girl Scouts.

"Trevor had it coming," Jade said. "Are you okay?"

I nodded, not quite sure how to respond. There was a minute of silence while Anji unpacked her lunch box and spread everything neatly on the table. Her lunch was extra-healthy. Carrot sticks and hummus. Some kind of homemade-looking bread.

"Jade says you're a superhero. Is that real?" she asked.

Jade had already shoved a handful of tater tots in her mouth, so her voice came out muffled. "I swear. It's true, right?"

I looked across the cafeteria at Kris. He and Trevor were cracking themselves up. Having a grand old time. He didn't seem to care at all that Trevor knew about the RLSH. Still. I wasn't going to tell anyone else.

"Look, she probably can't talk about it here," Jade said. She took a swig of chocolate milk and glanced around the lunchroom. "If we ask you questions, can you answer yes or no? We'll swear a solemn vow of secrecy."

Anji nodded so enthusiastically her twin braids bounced on her shoulders. "Good idea," she said. They touched their foreheads together and mumbled something about *knowledge to the grave*, a ritual they'd clearly done before. Then Anji jumped right in with the questions. "Okay, yes or no: Do you have a superhero name?"

I hesitated and Jade pushed Anji's shoulder playfully. "Of *course* she does. That question's too obvious. I'm sure it's something really cool. Zinnia has excellent taste."

Anji pushed her back. "I *know*." She rolled her eyes. Not

like she was annoyed. Or mad. Like it was a given. That *I* had excellent taste. In what?

The girls grinned at me and it was so bizarre. That they were sitting here. Wanting to talk to me. Thinking I was . . . cool? It snuck up on me and all of a sudden I laughed. If I'd had water in my mouth, I would have done a spit take.

"Yes," I said.

"*Yes* what?" Anji asked, and Jade shoved her again.

"*Yes*, she has a superhero name. She's playing the *game*, you dope!"

The girls started to giggle and this time I actually *did* have water in my mouth. I sprayed it all over the table. Some of it landed on Jade's tray. Which was disgusting, and suddenly, we were all laughing. All three of us. Together. Like friends. I still wasn't going to tell them anything about Kris or the Reality Shifters, but maybe it couldn't hurt to tell them about *me*.

"My superhero name is Spectrum," I said. "Like a rainbow."

"That makes total sense." Anji nodded. "You always wear rainbows. You've got your orange shirt on today. Yesterday was red. I like it that you go in order."

I stared at her. All this time, I'd thought I was invisible.

"You should see her costume," Jade said. "It has a rainbow cape."

"We call it a *gimmick*," I said.

I ended up telling them all about my gimmick, and the Wharf Patrol, and even about helping Pearl and Johanna get a taxi to Safe Harbor Women's Shelter.

"My cousin, Em, lives there!" Jade said. "She's a year younger than us. I wonder if she's seen Pearl?"

"Your cousin lives at Safe Harbor?" I asked.

"Yeah, I wish they could live with us, but our place is too small. Em says the other kids there are nice, though."

"Em's nice, too," Anji said. "You'd like her. She'll be with us in middle school next year."

"You'd *love* her," Jade said. "She's got great style, like you."

Before I knew it the bell was ringing and Jade and Anji were saying, "See you in L.A." and "Let's get ice cream this weekend." And I was saying, "Maybe." Because as much as I wanted to go get ice cream with these girls, I had a mission.

I'd just put away my lunch tray when I felt a tap on my shoulder.

"Hey, Zin." Kris was smiling, and I remembered that he'd been laughing all through lunch, too. With my nemesis. My smile disappeared.

"Trev asked me to give you this," he said. *Trev?* Were

they *friends* now? I tried to shrug it off. Kris could be friends with anyone he wanted, but Trevor? It felt like a betrayal.

He put a note in my hand and glanced over his shoulder. I followed his gaze to the back of the lunchroom where Trevor was standing, looking nervous.

"What does it say?" I asked. I wasn't sure I wanted to read it.

Kris shook his head. "No clue. I'm just the messenger."

I shoved the note in my pocket and turned to leave, but Kris lowered his voice, and said, "Hey, I have a question. About the mission."

Finally. I'd been wanting to talk to him about it all day.

"Do you think the surveillance is going to work?" Kris asked. "Or do you think we need some sort of a backup plan?"

"What do you mean? Why wouldn't it work?"

"Well, Trev was saying what if the thieves get away? It might be better if we had some kind of a plan, like a decoy laptop we could track or—"

My jaw practically came unhinged. First of all, of *course* the thieves weren't going to get away. There was a team of Real-Life Superheroes on patrol. Second of all—

"You *told* Trevor about the mission?"

Kris squirmed. "Not the *details*. It just . . . kinda came up."

I didn't even know how to respond. I gave Kris a tight smile. To be fair, I'd mentioned the mission to Jade and Anji . . . *and* I'd told them my superhero name. But that was different. They weren't known torturers with a proven ability to stick with the same joke for eight months straight.

"I think our plan is fine," I said. "I gotta go. See you in L.A."

I thought I'd wait until I got home to read Trevor's note. Or maybe I'd throw it out. Straight into the garbage. Where any message from Trevor Pryor belonged. But in reality, I only got through part of Spanish class before curiosity got the better of me. I propped up my textbook and snuck the note out of my pocket while the teacher was conjugating verbs. It felt so nice not to have someone whispering "Pollo Loco" in my ear. And still. I unfolded it.

Zinnia,

I'm sorry my chicken jokes made you feel bad. I thought they were funny, but I was wrong and I wish I could take it all back. I don't actually think you're a chicken. I think you're the nicest person in school. I understand if you don't forgive me.

Trevor

p.s. I found out who Wrecking Ball is!!!!! I promised I wouldn't tell, so I can't, but it's someone you'd never expect. Thanks for teaching me about the RLSH. How did you know about them anyway?

p.p.s. You don't have to write back if you don't want to.

p.p.p.s. I'm really sorry.

STING

Willow wasn't home when Dad dropped me off after school. Normally, if Mom has an afternoon shift, Dad brings me to the café before heading back to work. But Willow had promised she'd be there. She'd promised we'd look at the Powerhouse Café patrol schedule together. I dropped my backpack on the floor and tried not to feel like my heart had been squashed in a juicer. It was all right. Her stuff was still here. Half unpacked. That was good. Maybe she was going to show up any second.

I got out some crackers and peanut butter and sat down by the window in the living room, where I'd be able to see my aunt the second she came up the porch steps. Ekta's car was in the driveway, which meant Kris was home. Upstairs, I could hear him and Ekta banging around. But it didn't sound like elephant stomps. It sounded more like regular stuff. Cupboards and doors slamming. Then yelling, and someone stomping down the stairs.

I froze, listening. I'd never known Kris and Ekta to fight, or even get mad. I watched out the window, but whoever had run downstairs didn't go outside.

I heard a knock on the door.

"Zin? Are you home? Can I come in?"

When I heard what Kris was mad about, I went ballistic, too. Neither of us were on the surveillance schedule. The Reality Shifters weren't "comfortable" having me and Kris on Powerhouse patrol.

"What do you *mean* we're not on the list? It was *my* idea! They'd never even *know* about it if it wasn't for me!"

"She said we're too young." Kris grabbed a cracker and angrily slapped some peanut butter on it with the knife. "They're letting Sparrow do it, and he's only two years older than us!"

"We weren't too young to help them with everything else," I said. "We helped them give blankets to people who yelled at us. We helped them catch a *thief*!"

"It's not even night patrol." Kris was getting crumbs everywhere. "It's not fair!"

We stewed in silence for a minute, taking turns stabbing

the knife into the peanut butter. And then, even though I'd already decided not to ask the question, I blurted out the other thing that was bothering me.

"Why'd you sit with Trevor at lunch?"

Kris shrugged, like it wasn't that big a deal, but he kept his eyes on the table. "I wanted to talk to him about comics."

"You told him your superhero name?" I asked. "I thought you wanted to keep your identity secret."

"Wait." Kris looked at me, his eyebrows crumpled in disappointment. "Is that what he wrote in the note? He *told* you?"

"And why would you tell him about the mission?"

He slumped in his seat. "I don't know. He promised he wouldn't tell anyone. He seemed . . . different. Like *you*. So I believed him."

"People make promises all the time," I said. I didn't mean for it to sound so much like *I told you so*, but Kris's comment annoyed me. Trevor Pryor was nothing like me.

Kris moaned and put his head in his hand. I hadn't wanted him to feel miserable. A little bit bad, maybe. But that wasn't why I brought it up.

"Look, it's not as bad as you think." I took Trevor's note from my pocket and pushed it across the kitchen table toward Kris.

He unfolded it, and I watched his shoulders relax.

"He didn't tell you."

"I know." I wasn't exactly ready to forgive Trevor, but it mattered that he'd kept his promise to Kris. "I've been thinking about what he said about the decoy laptop. It's kind of smart, actually. Like a sting operation."

Kris looked surprised, but nodded. "Trev said he has a laptop with GPS tracking on it. So if you lose it, you can look it up on your phone and find the exact location on a map."

"It kind of stinks to say it," I said. "But he's really good at projects. He works superhard and he doesn't do stuff half-way." I winced thinking about it.

"What are you . . . ?" Kris raised his eyebrows at me.

"Do you have his phone number?" I asked reluctantly. When Kris nodded, I bit the bullet. "I think you should call him," I said. "Ask him to meet us at the café."

"Now?" Kris shook his head. "Mom would kill me. I'd be literally dead if I put on my gimmick and went on patrol right now."

"I know they don't want us on surveillance," I said. "But they can't stop us from visiting my mom. She works there, and I'm not supposed to be home alone anyway."

It wasn't the same as actually being on patrol with the other RLSH. But we could still help. At least we wouldn't be sitting at home twiddling our thumbs. Waiting around for people who promised they'd be there to never show up.

"Your aunt's at the café now, too," Kris said.

"She is?"

"It's on the schedule. Miles, Wheelie, and Sparrow until four thirty, Crystal Warrior and Mom until six thirty, and a couple of the eXtreme eXamples will take over until closing."

I checked the clock. It was almost three. "We *have* to go over there." I put the lid on the peanut butter. "Tell Trevor to bring the laptop, and put your gimmick in your backpack. Just in case."

"What am I going to tell my mom?" Kris asked. "She'll be suspicious."

"We're studying? You're staying for dinner? I don't know." I waved him away. "She's your mom. You figure something out."

While Kris went upstairs to call Trevor and get his gimmick, I changed into my rainbow tights, black dress, and Doc Martens, and put Ekta's silver whistle around my neck. I shoved my arm sleeves, mask, and cape into my backpack. I felt great about our plan. Prepared. Ready for anything.

Until we walked into the Powerhouse Café.

POWERHOUSE

The café looked the same as always. Almost every table was filled with people scrolling on their phones or typing on their laptops. Mom was at the espresso machine, steaming milk and chatting with Fatuma, who was refilling the coffee pots. My pace slowed as Kris and I walked toward the register. I'd sort of forgotten that Mom would notice me. Hanging out with Kris. Wearing Grandma's first-day-of-school dress.

Mom's lips immediately spread into a giant, unnatural smile. She was so excited, she could barely talk in her normal voice. I wanted to hide in the bathroom and never come out.

"Hi, Mom," I said.

"Hiiiiya, sweetie," she said in a ridiculous holding-in-her-joy voice. "You look *nice*. And *this* is . . . ?"

As if she didn't know.

"Kris," I said. "He lives upstairs. Remember?" My eyes shouted at her to knock it off, but she and Fatuma were too busy exchanging obvious looks to notice mine. They'd clearly been talking about me and my fake love life.

"Hi, Zinnia!" Fatuma actually winked at me. It was enough to make me want to abort the whole mission.

"Can we get some hot chocolates, please?" I asked.

"Yoooou *betcha*!" Even Kris, who'd never met my mom and couldn't know that this wasn't her normal behavior, was starting to look uncomfortable.

"So, what are you *two* doing this afternoon?" Fatuma emphasized the word *two* so much that I couldn't even look at her.

"Where's Willow?" Mom's smile faded a little. "I thought you were hanging out with her today?"

"I've got homework," I mumbled. My eyes drifted toward the window.

Kris nudged me, but I'd already seen them. Silver Sparrow and Wheelie were crossing the street. I didn't know how RLSH "surveillance" worked, but they'd clearly decided *not* to be inconspicuous. Wheelie high-fived a group of teenagers hanging out on the corner, and Sparrow stopped to ka-*kaw!* at a kid who was holding her mom's hand. I was pretty sure I saw Wheelie hand the lady a business card. Where was Miles? Hopefully, she got reassigned to a different time slot. This was not the kind of exciting crime patrol that was going to keep her interested in the RLSH.

"Two hot chocolates," Mom said, pushing the cups across the counter. She followed my gaze to the super-heroes and frowned.

Kris and I found a table near the window, but not too visible from the outside. I didn't want any of the Reality Shifters spotting us and trying to send us home.

"Whoa, your mom is really good at latte art." Kris pointed at the hot chocolates. Each of our drinks was topped with foam art. Two. Giant. Swirly. Hearts. I shot a glare across the room, but Mom was talking to Fatuma and didn't see me.

We got out our textbooks, and I actually did a few math problems while we waited for Trevor. But mostly I kept my eye on the window. Papa Wheelie and Silver Sparrow had moved out of sight. People walked up and down the street. A fluffy brown dog peed on a fire hydrant like a cliché. According to the schedule, Miles was supposed to be on patrol for another forty-five minutes. Did she not show up? I'd done my best to find an exciting mission, but maybe day patrol wasn't enough. Maybe I should have told her to sign up for night patrol with the eXtreme eXamples.

"Why don't your mom and Crystal like that other team?" I asked. "The eXtreme eXamples?"

"It's kind of stupid. There was a big fight."

"Really?" I imagined a full-on superhero battle. Capes flying in the wind. But Kris said it was a boring argument about crime patrol.

"Those guys think handing out food and supplies isn't superhero work," Kris said. "And Wheelie says *they* only want an excuse to wear bulletproof vests and look tough. So we quit and started our own league. We still team up with them sometimes, though."

"Do they?" I asked. "Look tough?"

"Tougher than us," Kris said.

"Who's tougher than you? No one!" The voice came from over my shoulder and I flinched at the sound of it.

"Trev!" Kris pulled a chair out, but Trevor Pryor didn't sit down. He didn't even set down his overfull blended ice drink with extra whipped cream. He looked at *me* first, like he wanted my permission.

"Hi," I said.

"Zinnia, I'm really sorry—" he started. He looked horrible. Like he hadn't slept. But I didn't feel like sitting through some awkward apology.

"I don't hate you," I said quickly. "And I'm sorry I yelled at you. But there are rules."

"Okay," Trevor said.

"No poultry jokes."

"Right." He stood there nodding while the whipped cream from his drink melted onto his laptop bag. I pointed to the empty chair, but he still didn't move.

"That's it," I said. "Just don't make fun of me. Or Kris. Or anyone."

"I promise." Trevor said it solemnly and made a cross-your-heart motion over his chest. It actually made me feel better. Trevor Pryor was the kind of person who followed through.

"I see why they picked this place." Trevor looked around the café as he sat down. "It's a 'risky facility' for sure."

"What are you talking about?" Kris asked. "It's a normal café."

"I have study hall for last period now instead of L.A. . . ." Trevor shot me a sheepish look and quickly added, ". . . which is *cool* because I got to do some research. People have been stealing laptops like this all over the world. It's usually a group of thieves and they raid a place all at once. They take stuff like phones and wallets, too, not just laptops."

He pulled a tiny notebook out of his bag and flipped to a page toward the end.

"They look for 'risky facilities,'" he said, reading off the page. "'Places that have more than one exit . . .'"

I looked around. Powerhouse had three exits. One at the front, one at the back by the bathrooms, and one behind us that led to a hallway and a side staircase.

"'. . . not a lot of staff . . .'"

Mom and Fatuma were the only ones who worked regularly. Half the time their after-school help didn't show up.

"'. . . no security cameras, tables close to doors, a path to the bathroom that passes by tables, and the busier the better. Obviously, you want a place where people come to use the Wi-Fi.' It looks like this place ticks off all those boxes, don't you think?"

Kris and I looked at each other.

"I told you," I said. "He's good at projects."

It wasn't that great a compliment, but Trevor beamed like I'd handed him a million dollars. He put the notebook on the table and unloaded the laptop. It was shiny and expensive-looking. I wondered if Ms. Pryor knew he was planning to use it as criminal bait.

"The best thing to do would be to leave the laptop unattended, but you have to do it naturally, like get up to go to the bathroom or something. Otherwise, it looks suspicious. We should wait till we see them, then we can implement the plan."

Here was the weak spot in our strategy.

"How are we supposed to know who they are? What if

they don't even come?" I scanned the packed room. There was a girl in all black with matching black earbuds sitting right next to the front door. A tattooed guy with a beard waiting for the bathrooms. A business-looking lady in a blazer who was glaring at the stairwell exit. It could be anybody.

"Watch and wait," Kris said. "To tell you the truth, I get why my mom doesn't like crime patrol. It's more boring than you'd think."

He wasn't kidding. By the time I'd finished my hot chocolate and Trevor had noisily sucked every last bit of crushed ice out of his plastic cup with his straw, Kris was leaning his chin on his hand in bored agony. He stared at his science book and let his head fall to the side, like he was falling asleep.

We were pretending to do homework, but we had Trevor's notebook in the center of the table and every time one of us saw something suspicious, we'd write a note to the others. *Pink shirt—trash can. Patriots jersey—back door. Spiked hair . . . bending toward that lady!*

None of them actually did anything incriminating. Pink Shirt threw out some napkins. Patriots Jersey held the door for an old lady. Spiked Hair kissed a girlfriend.

We'd started to play a tic-tac-toe tournament in the notebook when a teenage girl bumped me with her bulging tote bag. Her bright red lipstick made her face look ghostly white.

"Sorry," she said as she set her steaming cup of coffee on the next table over and squeezed into a chair too close to mine. Her long black hair smelled like one of those fruit shampoos the girls in my class like. I should know because she was sitting so close that when she flipped it over her shoulder, it whipped me in the face.

Trevor and Kris, already a little bonkers from boredom, lost it when they saw my shocked, hair-whipped expression. Several people, including the girl, turned to give our giggling table thank-god-I'm-not-in-middle-school looks.

Suddenly, Kris pulled it together and nudged my foot under the table.

Papa Wheelie and Silver Sparrow had showed up across the street again, with two more superheroes I'd never seen before. Both wore all-black gimmicks with bulletproof vests and black luchador-style masks that covered their whole heads except their mouths and chins. The four of them were clearly in a heated discussion. One of the new superheroes was waving her arms, pointing toward the roof of the building. She had a long blond braid down her back, and with the bulletproof vest and full-head mask, she looked kind of scary.

Kris rolled his eyes. "They always *do* this," he said. "We spend all this time making a plan and then the eXtreme eXamples ignore it and do what they want to do. They're supposed to wait until their shift."

I looked around the café to see if anyone else had noticed the superheroes arguing on the street, but most people were on their phones or computers, or focused on their conversations.

The fruity-haired girl next to me was texting on her phone. She was so close, I could read her messages over her shoulder.

Weirdos out front.

Good distraction?

"Are you guys done with these?"

Mom stood at our table and picked up our empty mugs. I cringed, waiting for her embarrassing Kris-related behavior to kick in, or worse, a bunch of awkward questions about Trevor, but she didn't shoot me a single knowing look or schmoopy smile. She was all business.

"Maria just clocked in, and I've asked her to make you more drinks. Two hot chocolates and a caramel blended ice?" Mom pointed to a teenager behind the counter steaming milk we hadn't asked for. Mom didn't even ask who Trevor was. Something was wrong.

"Thanks?" I said.

Mom stood with her back to the window, and I could tell from the way she was purposely *not* looking behind her that this was about the superheroes. Part of me wanted to explain the whole thing. Tell her that the reason they were out there was to *protect* her customers. That they were the good guys.

"I'm stepping out for a sec, and I need you to stay put. Okay, Zinnia?" She took a step back and accidentally kicked the fruity girl's tote bag. It clinked and the girl used her foot to pull it closer to her chair, still typing with her thumbs.

Where are you all?

Close.

Get here.

Mom went back to the counter and huddled up with Fatuma. Shook her head. Frowned. They didn't look happy. Fatuma got out her phone and held it to her ear.

I side-eyed the fruity girl's table. Her tote bag had fallen open and from my angle, I could see what had been clinking inside. Two tall aluminum cans. They looked exactly like the cans of red paint Kris had used to spray CUT ME! on the curb at the wharf.

The girl set her phone on the table while she took a drink of her coffee. On the bottom corner of her phone case was a small red X.

Trevor kicked my foot under the table. Had he seen it,

too? My heart sped up. But he wasn't kicking me about the girl.

"Zin." Kris jerked his head toward the window.

My mom and Fatuma were outside the café. Mom took a photo of the superheroes with her phone. Then they crossed the street toward the RLSH.

Out of the corner of my eye, I could see Maria leaving the counter with a massive tray full of drinks. She paused to call out a name and headed toward the back of the café to deliver one of the dozen mugs on her tray.

The girl next to me was typing fast with her thumbs.

No one at the register.

X marks the spot.

SURVEILLANCE

This was it. I could feel it. The moment the Real-Life Superheroes would rush in to save the day, and yet, I had a terrible, sinking feeling about the whole thing. First of all, Willow never showed. She was going to miss everything! And second of all, none of the RLSH were paying attention. Because Mom was distracting them.

"I have to talk to Mom," I said, pulling my backpack over my shoulder. I tried to move normally and sound casual, but I wagged my eyebrows frantically at Kris and Trevor. At least we had Trevor's laptop. If the thieves got away and took it back to their lair, or apartment, or whatever—we'd still be able to track them down.

"Okay, cool." Trevor was oblivious, thinking about his next tic-tac-toe move, but Kris got the hint. He scribbled

Now?? in one of the empty tic-tac-toe boxes and I gave a firm nod.

"We're on it," Kris said.

I caught up with Mom in time to hear her say, "You've been creeping around here all day and we've had enough, okay?"

"You're making our customers nervous," Fatuma said.

I frowned. It wasn't the customers who were nervous. It was Mom and Fatuma, and the people they *should* be nervous about were inside. Or at least one of them was, and more were on the way. Maybe it was better Willow wasn't here after all. Mom was already mad enough. Her head would seriously explode if she knew my aunt and I were part of this. She wouldn't understand.

"We're out here keeping the neighborhood safe, ma'am," Papa Wheelie said. He shot her a smile. Too bad he didn't know how much Mom hates being called *ma'am*.

"Can you help another neighborhood, please?" Fatuma asked. "We're trying to run a business."

"Sorry, ladies." The woman in black stepped forward. Her voice was strong. Intimidating. Like an army general. "Our mission is *here*."

"Mom, they're here to help," I said.

For once, Mom's hawkeye had missed something. She

was so busy worrying about the RLSH that she hadn't noticed I'd followed her across the street.

"Zinnia's right," Silver Sparrow said. "We're here to protect you."

"Exactly." Papa Wheelie reached out and patted my arm in solidarity. Mom froze. I knew what she was thinking. Some old man in a mask was touching her daughter.

She glanced back at the café. In time to see one more superhero in an all-black gimmick disappear down the alley. This was not what we needed. The eXtreme eXamples might be tough, but did they have to look so scary?

"I've already reported this incident to the police," Fatuma said.

"You don't understand!" I said. "The people we're looking for are inside!"

I expected Wheelie or Silver Sparrow to leap into action. Race toward the café. Apprehend the thieves. But no one seemed to understand what I meant—the people we were looking for were inside *now*. Not theoretically. Actually.

There was a quick whistle from the direction of the café. Specifically, from the direction of the roof. Where I caught a glimpse of a fedora. Miles must have found a way to get up there after all. Rooftop surveillance. Even with Mom gearing up to ruin things, I couldn't help but smile.

But the whistle was a warning.

A police car rolled up to the sidewalk. Nice and slow. No lights or sirens. Both front doors opened at the exact same time and two officers got out of the car. One of them rolled his eyes when he saw the superheroes. The other took out a notebook and clicked her pen.

"We had a report of a disturbance," she said. "Are these folks bothering you?"

"No!" I said. "They're not! But there are criminals—"

"Zinnia." Mom grabbed my elbow. "I need you to go back inside."

To the police officer, Fatuma said, "Yes, these are the people I called about."

"All right," the officer said, waving her notebook toward the RLSH. "Let's take this comic-book convention somewhere else, okay?"

Papa Wheelie started to calmly explain that they weren't here to bother anyone, but the woman from the eXtreme eXamples got all huffy.

"You can't make us leave." She crossed her arms and repeated it. The third time she said it, the policeman reached for his radio.

"Hey, StarLight," Papa Wheelie scolded the woman in black. "Lay off. Cut the theatrics."

But StarLight was on a roll now, lecturing the police officers about free speech and inalienable rights and the next thing we knew, another member of the eXtreme eXamples was jogging out of the alley and crossing the street.

"Star," he called out, raising a hand. He'd obviously seen her get worked up like this before, and he didn't seem happy about it. "Calm it down a notch, okay?"

He was clearly trying to help, but seeing a masked superhero in a bulletproof vest running across the street only made Mom, Fatuma, and the police more nervous. I could see why Ekta didn't want the eXtreme eXamples involved.

Papa Wheelie shook his head and threw his hands in the air.

"Come on, Sparrow," he said. "If these jokers want to get arrested, let 'em. Next time I suggest a team-up, knock me unconscious, okay?"

But as he turned his chair to leave, Mom gasped.

"Wait!" she said. "Officer, they might have something to do with the graffiti we reported on our building, too."

"What?" I gaped at her. I hadn't realized Mom had seen the red X, too. But she had it all wrong.

"We didn't have anything to do with that," I said. "The person who *did* is in the café." I tried hard to keep my voice calm. Cool. Collected. Explain the situation. Then she'd see.

"There's a girl inside who seems really suspicious and I think she's texting her friends."

But Mom didn't see. "*We*? What are you talking about, Zinnia?"

The policeman moved his hand toward his belt. "We did get a suspicious phone call from a 'superhero' regarding graffiti on this building," he said.

"That wasn't suspicious," I said. "We were *trying* to help. You're not listening."

"*Zinnia.*" Mom's voice got extra-quiet but her eyes were screaming at me. "Go back to the café. *Now.*"

My brain told me to go. I'd be in huge trouble if I didn't. But I couldn't move. The policewoman had already gone through the pockets of Wheelie's chair and found two cans of red spray paint. They clinked together as she pulled them out.

"That's it," the police officer said, gesturing at the RLSH. "You're coming in for questioning." She turned toward Papa Wheelie. Sparrow looked nervous. Scared. "How many more 'superheroes' are around here?" she asked.

No one answered, so the officer pulled out her radio and spoke into it. "Can I get someone to sweep the area around Powerhouse Café?"

She'd barely finished the sentence when the shouting started.

Someone inside the café yelled, and then someone else. A couple guys holding skateboards and backpacks left out the side door and walked down the alley. They passed another black-clad member of the eXtreme eXamples who was running our way, yelling, "Mission control! Mission control!"

Fatuma gasped.

The front door opened, and Kris and Trevor sprinted across the street. "Someone stole the cash register," Kris panted. "We tried to get to him, but it was too crowded. He went out the back."

Trevor had his laptop bag slung around his shoulder. It looked heavy. Heavier than it should. The laptop inside it was supposed to be gone.

"What happened?" I asked.

"They didn't take it." He looked terrified. "We left it on the table but it was really crowded. They only took stuff from people in the back."

I felt horrible. This was my fault. My mission. My mom messing everything up.

People were starting to come out of the café, rushing toward the police to tell them what had happened.

"Someone took my purse!" a lady yelled.

"My laptop," a guy called.

"My phone!"

"I saw someone in a black mask through the window . . . he looked like that!"

Two men in the alley were tussling with an eXtreme eXample. "We caught one!" one of the men yelled as they dragged the superhero across the street toward the police. At the very same moment that Crystal Warrior showed up in her gimmick, a whole half hour early for her patrol. The look on her face when she saw the scene outside the Powerhouse made everything crystal clear: my mission was a disaster.

While the police were busy loading superheroes into the patrol car, the girl with long black hair exited the café. She walked right out the front door. Casual. Talking on the phone.

"That's her!" I pulled on Mom's arm and tried to get the policewoman's attention. No one even looked at me.

Except the fruity-haired girl. She glanced in my direction. Flipped her long hair over her shoulder. Adjusted her tote bag. And walked, slowly and calmly, away.

THE CAT

It only took one more look from Mom before I grabbed Kris and Trevor and headed for the café. Once inside, I went straight for the back door.

"Where are we going?" Trevor asked.

"The roof."

"Right," Kris said. "They're going to look for more RLSH. We can tell them to clear out. Do you think our team caught *any* of the thieves? There had to be at least five or six. They moved so fast!"

"It was bananas," Trevor said. "One of them actually *picked up* the cash register and ran with it. How heavy must that be? One man tried to stop him but the thief shoved the register at him and pushed him—"

I interrupted. "If we hurry, we might be able to see where she went!"

"Who?"

"The ringleader. It's the girl who hit me with her hair!"

I appreciated that Kris and Trevor didn't argue. They didn't ask for proof. They trusted that I knew what I was talking about and quickly followed me out the back door.

When Trevor saw the fire escape, he hesitated. I didn't blame him. The fire escape ladder in the back of the Powerhouse Café was intimidating—at least twice as tall as the one leading up to Kris's window at One Ocean Avenue.

"I don't think I have the ability to do that," Trevor said. "Sorry . . . just being honest."

"Be our lookout," Kris said. "We'll be back down as soon as we can."

Kris let me go up the fire escape first so I wouldn't be so afraid of falling. Which I was. Very. Afraid.

I put hand over hand, and forced myself to take deep breaths. My legs shook, and I tried not to imagine how far down the pavement was. Or how hard. Still. Even with the fear, and even without my superhero gimmick, I felt strong. I could hear Kris's shoes hitting the metal rungs below me. His voice cheering me on.

"You're good, Zin," he said. "You've got this."

Zin.

It was nice. Having someone around who called me that.

Miles and a guy in an eXtreme eXamples gimmick reached toward the ladder and helped us up the last few steps.

"Zinnia, how are you so brave?" Miles asked. She was blushing. "We saw the chaos, but I got too scared to climb down the fire escape, and the door to the stairs is locked. I'm a total superhero failure."

She gave an embarrassed laugh. Like she didn't actually feel like a failure. Like she was having a blast.

"There are *stairs*?" I was so glad to put my feet on something resembling a floor. I'd never been on a roof before, and thankfully, it wasn't as scary as I'd expected. More like a patio with a waist-high brick wall around it. There were even a few plants and some lawn chairs up there.

The man with Miles chuckled and pointed to a door on the other end of the roof where an eXtreme eXample with long curly hair was picking the lock.

When Kris stepped onto the roof, he high-fived the man in black.

"Hey, Scar!"

"Wrecking Ball!" The guy grinned. He had a scar across the bottom of his dark brown chin that looked oddly familiar.

"Derek?" I asked. "You're RLSH?" No wonder he knew so much about the Reality Shifters. "But I thought—"

"Good to see you, Rainbow!" Scar said. "We kinda missed all the action, but lucky thing Jewels and I were here to save your aunt from this rooftop."

"What is Jen doing?" my aunt asked me. "Is she getting those guys arrested? Did I just see them handcuff Papa Wheelie?"

I didn't have time to answer. I ran toward the side of the roof and peered over the edge.

"What're you looking for?" Scar followed me to the side of the building.

"We need to stay out of sight," Kris said. "The police are looking for more RLSH. They think we're the thieves."

"But we're not," I said. "That girl is!"

I pointed to a spot a block away, where the girl was strolling down the sidewalk, her tote bag snugged up to her side.

"That girl? Heading toward Memorial Park?" Miles asked.

"She planned the whole thing," I said. "I saw her texts." I glanced around but I didn't see anyone else who looked like they were running away with stolen goods. Or cash registers. I wondered if the rest of them had getaway cars.

"Doesn't seem like she's in any rush," Scar said. "She's a slick cat."

She did look a little catlike, the way she walked all confident, with her secret, toward the park.

"Let's do it!" Miles said, tipping her fedora in my direction. "I need to redeem myself. Let's catch the Cat." She said it like the girl was a Real-Life Supervillain. With a code name. Like us.

"We need our costumes," Kris said, frantically looking around for a place to change.

"*Gimmicks*," I said, teasing him. "We don't have time."

The curly-haired superhero finished her work on the lock and we all took the stairs down to the first floor. Which was way less scary than climbing the metal fire escape. But when Scar opened the door that led into the café, a police officer was waiting inside. He said something into his radio and motioned for Scar to follow him.

"Plus the other two," the officer said. "Come on out."

The other two. Maybe it was because we were kids. Or because we were in our plain clothes. Either way, the police officer only had his eye on the superheroes. I pulled Kris farther away from them and pretended to look at the drinks menu. As the others followed the police officer out of the café, Miles slipped me her phone.

"Don't get too close, but try to get a photo," she whispered. "I'll make sure someone calls Ocean for backup."

"What?" I asked. She expected me and Kris to catch the Cat on our *own*?

"You can do this, Spectrum. Don't let her get away."

She grinned at me. Even now, with the police and my mom about to read her the riot act, she was having the time of her life. Well, good. At least one of us was.

"She's right," Kris said. "All we need to do is get a photo. Then the police can identify her."

I shoved Willow's phone in the pocket of my dress and we ran for the back door. The Cat had been heading toward the park, and she hadn't seemed in any hurry. If we ran the whole way, maybe we could catch up with her. All we had to do was get a photo, like Willow said. Let the police identify her. Then they could break up the whole operation. How hard could a photo be?

Trevor was waiting at the fire escape, as promised. He looked confused to see us come out the back door.

"How'd you get in there?" he asked.

"We gotta go. Come on!" Kris said, but before we started jogging, Trevor slowed us down.

"Wait. Go where? I can't." He held up a cell phone. "I called my mom. She's calling the police to explain, and then she's coming to meet us here. To help."

I'd been wrong. Trevor wasn't good at projects. He was great at them. If anyone knew how to convince the police *and* talk some sense into my mom, it was Ms. Pryor.

"Good call," I said. "But we can't wait. Meet us at Memorial Park when your mom gets here."

We didn't hear his response because Kris and I took off as fast as two sixth graders without superpowers could go. It wasn't lightning speed, but it was close enough.

FIGHTING CRIME

When Kris and I crossed the street to Hilltop Memorial Park, the Cat was already near the playground, only a block from One Ocean Avenue. The singing man was on the swing set belting out a song, as always, and his aide read a book on a nearby bench. The elderly lady with the black pug was there, tossing a ball that her dog refused to fetch. Farther down, there was a guy running, and a couple with a baby stroller walked up the hill from the beach.

The Cat kept checking her phone and hadn't seemed to notice she was being followed, which was a good thing. I tried snapping a few photos as we walked, but it was hard to get the phone's camera to focus. All the shots I was getting were too far away, plus they were all pictures of the back of her head. That wasn't going to be very helpful.

Maybe it was because I was in Memorial Park, on home turf, surrounded by all the memories of people who'd been loved and missed, but I suddenly felt a surge of bravery. Like I was standing at the wharf with a whole team of super-heroes circled up with me.

I jumped up on a bench. *In loving memory of Eloise (1954–2002).*

"What are you doing?" Kris whispered.

Standing on the bench, I could see someone on the porch of One Ocean Avenue. I waved my arm in case it was Ocean, ready to spring into superhero action. Ready to save us the second anything went wrong.

"Excuse me!" I shouted in the direction of the Cat. Bold. Loud. All we needed was a photo. "Excuse me, miss! I think you dropped something."

I got ready and as the girl turned to face us, her hair whipped through the air like a cheesy commercial. I snapped a photo. Several photos. I knew I was catching her perfectly. Her surprise. Her look of recognition when she saw me and Kris. She definitely remembered us from the café.

I don't know what I thought was going to happen after I got the photo. I guess I thought we'd bolt. Run toward One Ocean Avenue like our feet had wings. We'd find Ekta. Get the photos to the police. I thought when she saw us taking pictures, the Cat would run away with her tail between her legs.

I was right about one thing. The Cat did run. In *our* direction.

"Hey!" she yelled. Meaner than I'd thought she could. She dropped her bag and I suddenly noticed how strong she looked. And how angry. "Are you taking my *picture*?"

I barely had time to hop off the bench as she lunged toward me, grabbing for Aunt Willow's phone.

I tried to dart out of the way, but she reached for my arm, pulling my sleeve until I heard the fabric under the armpit tear.

Before she could get any closer, Kris dropped to the ground and rolled himself into the Cat's path. She tripped over his body and tumbled to the ground, her long hair flying as Kris kept rolling out of the way. I stared, frozen in place. It was a serious superhero move. But it had only made the Cat madder.

"Run! Home!" Kris said as the girl stood up, red-faced and ready to explode.

I'd only run a few feet toward One Ocean Avenue when she yelled, "Give me that phone!" and something hard hit the heel of my foot. I fell to the grass, next to a can of red spray paint the Cat had thrown at me. I could barely think. Five feet away, a supervillain's anger was exploding. At me.

I felt Ekta's whistle around my neck and even though I didn't know if it would do any good, I brought it to my lips and blew my lungs out. Over and over. Like that little girl Pearl had done when I'd wanted to get Ocean's attention. Only that time, all we needed was for Ocean to help us get Pearl and her family to a safe place. We didn't have a super-villain towering over us. Reaching for the phone in my hand. Pulling at my whistle until the cord dug into the back of my neck. I closed my eyes and I knew it didn't actually make sense but part of my brain was stuck on two words: *if only*. If only I had my gimmick. If only Aunt Willow was here. If only we'd never left Wisconsin. If only I had my brother.

I'd be stronger.

The whistle's cord stopped digging into my neck, and at first I thought it had broken. But it hadn't. When I opened my eyes, I could see that the Cat had let go because Kris had rolled into her legs again, knocking her to the ground. They were both on their backs. I blew the whistle one more time as Kris grabbed one of the Cat's arms and hugged it, then threw one leg over her head and the other over her chest, pinning her to the ground.

Suddenly, I realized we weren't alone. The whistle had

worked! Next to Kris, the black pug appeared, growling and gripping the Cat's sleeve with its teeth. Next to the pug stood the old woman. The singing man and his aide. The runner and the couple with the baby stroller. Ekta was there. And somehow, even my dad. They'd all heard my whistle, and they'd circled up, forming a wall around me, Kris, and the girl with the fruity hair. Like a bunch of real-life superheroes. Only not one of them was wearing a gimmick. Not even a mask.

Trevor and Ms. Pryor were there, too. Trevor reached out to help me up, and I took his hand.

I would have thought I was dreaming, but the man from the swings started singing "Somewhere Over the Rainbow." And the singing was so loud and so out of tune it had to be real. It was beautiful.

STORIES

I'd been right about one thing. The Reality Shifters were in the news again after we caught the Cat. And not just once. The *Port City Times, Southern Maine Weekly,* even *Boston* magazine—it seemed like within twenty-four hours, every single newspaper, TV channel, radio station, and Internet zine had shown up at One Ocean Avenue, wanting an interview with the Real-Life Superheroes. I wasn't allowed to talk to the reporters. Not that I wanted to. Aunt Willow stayed in our bedroom listening to Miles Davis and packing all her stuff. Again.

We could hear Ocean, Crystal Warrior, and Papa Wheelie on the front lawn, giving speeches to the reporters. As usual, Crystal Warrior did most of the talking. She was trying out a new tagline. Instead of *Hope for the hopeless. Help for the helpless*, she used *Extreme altruism*, which I liked a lot better because it didn't make people like Derek and Johanna seem powerless. Harper and Kris tried to check in on me, but my parents told them I was grounded. Permanently. So Harper slipped a silly cartoon under the door. It was a drawing of all of us in our gimmicks with one giant speech bubble that said, *Ka*-kaw! At least it was good to see them all through the window.

After the Powerhouse patrol, stories popped up all over the Internet about the RLSH. Some headlines made us out to be heroes who'd saved the day. "Citizen Activists Take a Stand Against Crime" and "Real-Life Superheroes Keep Port City Safe." But just as many were titled "Costumed Crew Interrupts Police Investigation," "Masked Madness Puts Kids in Danger," and "Has the Superhero Craze Gone Too Far?"

Dad created a story, too. When he'd picked Willow up from the police station, she introduced him to Derek. It turned out he got offered the job he'd interviewed for, but when the employer found out Derek didn't have a place to live, the company decided to give the position to someone else. When Dad heard that, he pulled out his recorder right there on the spot. His story wasn't about the superheroes. It was about discrimination and the long wait lists for shelters and housing assistance. Dad's boss thought the story was so important that he assigned him a whole series about homelessness and food insecurity in Port City, with a stipend for Derek as an associate producer. So Dad felt like, finally, he was shining a light on something that mattered. But no one else in our house was happy. At all.

It didn't make any sense. We'd captured a ring of serial criminals. Kept them from hitting more shops in the future. That was a good thing. Indisputably good. Heroic, even. We should be celebrating with pizza and root beer.

Instead, Mom forgot everything she'd ever said about forgiving Aunt Willow. Before I even had a chance to explain about the RLSH and why we had joined, Mom booked Willow a plane ticket to Wisconsin. For Saturday morning.

"That's not fair!" I tried to argue, but Mom held up her hand.

"She put your *life* in danger, Zinnia." It was almost a whisper, but I could hear her rage. Bits and pieces. Bones and hair.

Even *after* I'd explained about the day patrols and the blankets and helping people get to safe places, both Mom and Dad banned me from ever participating in a Reality Shifters patrol again.

"What if I promise not to do crime-fighting anymore?" I begged. "What if I only did the other stuff? The Saturday patrols. I like that better anyway. *Please.*"

Mom didn't even bother to answer. She blinked at me like she didn't know who I was. Like she'd never seen me in her life. All Dad said was no.

My whole life felt like it had exploded, but on Friday, at Oceanside Middle School, we did math equations and practiced verbs in Spanish like it was any other day. Some of the kids buzzed about fake superheroes they'd seen in the news, but Kris, Trevor, and I were only ever referred to as "three local minors." Everyone's guess was that they were kids from St. Mark's. Probably something had leaked about Silver Sparrow. The only ones who had a clue were Jade and Anji.

"Was that *you*?" Anji whispered at lunch. "Don't worry, we're still sworn to secrecy."

Jade could barely sit still, waiting for my answer. I don't know why, but I didn't want to talk about the mission. Not with Willow leaving because of it. Not with me being banned from the team.

"I can't talk about it yet," I said. "Superheroes' code."

In Mr. Iftin's class, I was supposed to finish "How to Be a Real-Life Superhero" all on my own. Trevor and I had finished the sections *How to Find Your Superhero Name* and *How to Create a Gimmick*. But I was only halfway through *How to Build a Team*. I felt like giving up. Taking an "incomplete" on the project didn't seem like that big a deal in the scheme of things. What was the point? My patrolling days were over. Mom had made that extra-clear. Besides. In the end, it hadn't been the superheroes who caught the Cat after all. It was me, plain old Zinnia. And Kris, not Wrecking Ball. Ms. Pryor and Trevor. Plus Dad, and Ekta, and all the people in the park who'd helped us out. Regular people. The pug.

"You want help?" Kris pulled his desk a little closer. "I finished mine. And I *might* know a thing or two about superheroes."

He grinned at me. The whole Powerhouse debacle hadn't gone over the same on the second floor of One Ocean Avenue. In fact, Ekta thought it went great. After the Cat got apprehended and taken down to the police station, Ekta followed behind to make sure the other superheroes got released. By that time, Emilia had already talked the Port City chief of police into setting up a meeting with the whole team, to brainstorm ways the Reality Shifters could most effectively help the city. Not only did the chief listen to her, he even assigned an officer to be an "RLSH Liaison" so Emilia would have a contact person on speed dial and the police and the superheroes could always be on the same page. Kris was excited about all of that, too, but he was mostly buzzing because he'd gotten to try out his favorite jiu-jitsu move in real life.

"It's called an arm bar," he said, practically bouncing in his chair. "I've been practicing it every night for months, and it worked! My mom's harder to take down than that woman was, for sure."

Jiu-jitsu practice. The nighttime thumping and banging.

"We thought that was elephants," I said, and Kris gave me a funny look. I frowned.

"I'm sorry you can't be on the team anymore," he said. "Maybe your parents will come around. Once they cool off."

I shook my head. He didn't know my parents. Honestly, I didn't mind giving up crime patrol one bit. When it wasn't boring, it was terrifying. I didn't need to chase down angry criminals. Once was more than enough. I *was* going to miss the stuffing parties, though. And Saturdays. It felt great having a team. Making a difference with socks, burrosas, and smiles.

"Maybe if you show them your project," Kris said, pointing to the page I was working on, "they'll think about it differently."

"Maybe," I said.

My eyes stayed on the page title for a minute. *How to Build a Team.* I looked across the room to where Anji and Jade were working, heads bent over their paper, giggling. They'd sat with me at lunch again. Like it was no big deal. A normal thing they did every day. We'd talked about super-heroes a little, but mostly about gelato and how Jade's little brother kept sneaking around and hiding rubber snakes in her bed.

"Maybe . . ." I said again.

Actually, the wheels in my brain were turning. It was almost miraculous that somewhere among the wreckage, there was a race car speeding down one of my neural path-ways. *Let's* tryyyy *it again!* I'd been thinking all day about Wally and the stories we'd made together. All those stories I'd lost at the bottom of the lake. Whenever we finished a story, if he didn't like the ending, Wally would say, "New story!" He didn't want a new story, really, just a new ending. "Too late, Wally. That's the way it ends," I'd say. But Wally wouldn't believe me. He said there were a thousand end-ings. It was our job to keep starting over until we found the right one.

"Maybe they'd let us start a new team," I said. "Like a club. At school."

Kris looked skeptical.

"We could organize food drives," I said. "Collect coats and mittens."

"Would we wear our gimmicks?"

I thought about it. We hadn't needed our gimmicks to catch the Cat. In fact, there wasn't anything the Reality Shifters had done that we couldn't have accomplished in regular clothes. I remembered what Papa Wheelie had told us in the van. None of us were *heroes*. We weren't swooping in to save the day. That's not what it was about. It was about regular people, shining a light. Seeing a problem, and lending a helping hand. In supercool costumes.

"We wouldn't *have* to wear the gimmicks," I said. "But it's way more fun."

Kris grinned, getting interested. "Halloween's coming up," he said. "We could do a candy drive."

I imagined showing up in superhero costumes to Safe Harbor. Bringing candy to Pearl, if she and her mom were still there. And getting to meet Jade's cousin, Em. It wasn't the same as being part of the Reality Shifters, and it wouldn't keep Aunt Willow in Maine. But it was something. A start, maybe.

"I bet Jade and Anji would join. And . . ." I paused, thinking over whether I really meant it. I decided I did. "We could invite Trevor. Maybe we could do more things, too. Bigger things."

"Like what?"

"I don't know," I admitted. "We'd have to think it over. But Jade said even here at Oceanside, there are kids who don't have permanent homes or enough to eat. I bet a lot of people would help if they had something specific they knew they could do."

We spent the rest of class planning out our Heroes Club instead of working on my project, but really I figured it was all part of the same thing.

Before I left school, I stopped in the office and knocked on Ms. Pryor's door.

"I'm glad to see you, Zinnia!" Ms. Pryor's smile was so bright it felt like a warm hug.

"Thanks for helping us," I said. "It was really smart of Trevor to call you."

Ms. Pryor smiled and waited. Like she knew that wasn't the reason I'd come.

"I was hoping I could come talk to you sometimes?" I asked. I couldn't keep myself from staring at my boots. "I have a free period on Tuesdays."

Honestly, a few months ago, that would have sounded like prison. Back in Wisconsin, sitting in the school counselor's office meant suffering through sad looks and uncomfortable questions. But Ms. Pryor was different. Talking to her had made me feel lighter. Stronger.

"You were right about saying things out loud," I said. "It helps."

"And asking for what you need," Ms. Pryor added. "I'll look forward to seeing you on Tuesday."

Halfway out the door, I turned back. I had one more request.

"May I have a piece of chocolate?"

IN A SILENT WAY

When Dad drove me home from school, we found Mom and Willow sitting at the kitchen table. Willow was leaving in the morning, so even though they were still mad, both Mom and Dad had taken the afternoon off. I set down my backpack carefully, bracing for another argument, but my mom and aunt weren't fighting. They were laughing and drinking tea, their heads bent over a book. Dad sat down at the table next to Mom, and when I stepped closer, Aunt Willow handed me a book, too.

"I made these a long time ago," she said. "I was going to give them to you on Sunday, but . . ."

You're leaving.

I sat down at the table and looked at the cover of the book. It was one of those hardcover photo books you can order online and it had a picture of my brother on the front. In Aunt Willow's graduation cap. Crossing his eyes and sticking out his tongue. The title read: *The Fabulous Adventures of the Mystical Walleye.*

I peeked over at Mom's book before opening mine. She had hers open to a collage with six different photos of Mom and Wally reading his favorite book, *Zin! Zin! Zin! a Violin.* In the first photo, he was tiny. Two years old, maybe, with a head of wild curls. Mom was trying to pull the book away from him because he had one corner of it in his mouth. In the last photo, he was maybe five or six, much more grown up, in a striped shirt, but he still looked tiny, because he was squashed on the couch between me, Mom, and Aunt Willow.

"Look at your hair!" I couldn't help laughing. I'd forgotten about the terrible perm Willow had gotten in high school. "You look like you got zapped by lightning."

Willow smiled, and Mom tapped her finger on the photo. Wally was grinning ear to ear. He had the exact same smile as Aunt Willow.

"Wally made me read that book at least once a day," Mom said. "I probably have it memorized."

"Remember how he used to conduct his animal orchestra?" Dad asked.

Willow and I both started mimicking Wally at the same

time. Hands swinging in the air, giving an extra flourish toward the stuffed-animal elephants in the back row. He would throw an imaginary fit if he thought the giraffe wasn't playing the cymbal at the right time.

My book was filled with photos of me and Wally. Building sandcastles. Doing magic tricks. Putting on plays. I paused on a full-page photo of the two of us in our canoe. Wally was wearing the same striped shirt he was wearing in Mom's photo and he had all his hair. Which meant the photo must have been taken the summer *before*. Before we knew about the tumor. Before Aunt Willow disappeared. Before Captain Walleye steered us full speed into a tsunami of piranhas and I left all our stories to disintegrate on the bottom of the lake.

I stared at the photo. The canoe tied to the dock. Wally, pretending to steer. Me, head down, taking notes. The historian. *New story*, I thought. Only I didn't want a new story. Just a new ending. One where my brother didn't end up in the hospital. At all.

I tried to tell myself the same old things.

It wasn't a big deal.

It was a long time ago.

Sometimes, sad things happen and there's nothing you can do but move on.

"ZZ, are you okay?"

Willow, Mom, and Dad were looking at me. Leaning forward. Watching my tears drop all over the canoe, my book, and into the lake.

"I told him he was stupid." It felt horrible even to whisper it. Like I was opening the door and letting in something I shouldn't. Something dark. And mean. I needed a power move, like Kris's arm bar, to knock it to the ground. Pin it down. Push it away. But it was stronger than me. "It's the last thing I said to him. I was mad that he tipped the canoe, and that's the last thing I said."

My cheeks felt hot, but the tears dripping down felt hotter.

Mom scooted close and put her arms around me. She was crying, too. So was Dad. And Willow.

"I wish I'd put that canoe away," Dad said. "It was too cold. It was my fault. I should have put it away in August."

Mom shook her head. "I should have been watching the kids more closely. I could have stopped it. I wasn't paying attention."

She was so close that her breath got tangled in my hair, and for a moment, I held perfectly still. I'd never heard my parents say those things before. We'd all been there when the doctor promised that the ice-cold lake had nothing to do with any of it. We'd all heard him say it. One hundred percent. A coincidence. A fluke. Why was that so hard to believe? After all this time, I still felt like it was my fault. But I hadn't known that Mom and Dad did, too.

Quietly, Willow got up from the table and went into our bedroom. My bedroom. I had to get used to the fact that she was leaving in the morning. I figured she didn't want to be at the table with a bunch of crying people anymore. *Fine.*

But when she came back out, she was carrying her guitar and her amplifier.

"This is the song," she said, "that I was going to play."

She sat on the floor in the living room and nodded for us to move to the couch. I sat in the middle, with Mom and Dad close on either side. I could feel them breathing, chests rising in unison, as Aunt Willow started to play.

It was the song from the *Panthalassa* album: "In a Silent Way." I recognized it even though it was different from the version we'd heard when Willow and I were creating our gimmicks. There wasn't any superhero hum in the beginning, just a quiet, sad melody. It filled the room and settled over me, and just like I had the first time I'd heard it, I thought of Cygnus the Swan. For a moment, I felt like I was underwater. Like I couldn't get a breath. Diving. Searching. Feathers sprouting.

But as the melody built and grew, something else took hold. Instead of feeling pinned down, my body started to relax. The music lifted and soared, and my heart lifted with it. It wasn't a burning sphere made of fiery gas. Not a star fixed in the sky. It was a real, live, beating heart. Free to move. And grow. As Willow's song surrounded it, I felt my heart swell until it was big enough to hold everything. Then. And now. Before. And after. Wally. The Reality Shifters. Aunt Willow. No matter where she was. I had all of it with me. Now.

Mom and Dad reached across me to hold hands, and I wondered if Willow's music was making their hearts grow, too. Sitting between them, it felt like it. It felt like all around us, there was room for hope.

This wasn't the end of the story. I didn't have to start over. I didn't have to erase Wally and start new.

All I had to do was continue our adventures.

OCEANSIDE OPTIMISTS

"That's the thing about capes," I said. I tried to make my voice sound extra nice so Anji—aka Snow Angel—wouldn't feel like I was bossing her around. "They're more dangerous than you'd think, but don't worry. All we need are some magnets. We can fix it."

Anji's gimmick was really cool. All white with gold and silver accents. Jade's was the total opposite. Black on black with a hint of pale purple. Nightshade. It was a great name. Though Kris said she shouldn't use it because there was already a Marvel superhero named Nightshade, and then Trevor said actually DC Comics had a Nightshade character, too, and *that* started a discussion of which Nightshade would win in a battle. I handed them another box of donations to sort while they talked.

"I don't think it matters," Jade said, adding the last of the shampoo bottles to her backpack. "It's not like I'm going to sell Nightshade T-shirts or anything."

Kris and Trevor stopped sorting supplies and stared at each other before blurting, "We should make T-shirts!" at the exact same time.

When we finished stuffing our backpacks, I sat down at the table at the front of Mr. Iftin's classroom, opened my journal to a blank page, and cleared my throat. Jade, Anji, Trevor, and Kris kept talking about gimmicks and super-heroes. Anji couldn't stop twirling and flapping her arms in her Snow Angel cape. At first, it had felt strange to be in the Language Arts room after hours, but now that I'd gotten used to it, I liked having the place to ourselves. I liked that we were in charge. I tapped my pencil on the table, but nobody noticed. Kris belly laughed at something Trevor said.

"You guys!" I said. Loud enough for Mr. Iftin, our after-school-club adviser, to pop his head into the classroom to make sure we were fine. I grinned at him. "I'm starting the meeting! We've got to be ready before they get here!"

When everyone had taken a place at the table, I went over my notes in my journal.

"Did everyone think about Jade's idea?" I asked. "About

the Oceanside Free Fashion Room? I talked to Mr. Iftin about it, and he said he could help us find a room in the school where people can drop off donations. We'll sort everything, and students can pick out free clothes whenever they need them. It'll be open to anyone who wants to use it. Ms. Pryor said she'd help us, too."

"Could we set it up like a store?" Jade asked. "So it's fun to shop in?"

"I thought we could ask people to donate more than just clothes," Anji said. "Like the kind of stuff we're bringing on the mission today. Toothpaste and toilet paper. Feminine supplies. You know?"

"Yeah, and snacks and food for the weekend?" Kris added.

"I could do some research and compile a list of the most useful items," Trevor said.

"And we could ask what people actually need," I added. "So we know we're collecting stuff that's really going to make a difference."

"I bet my cousin, Em, would help," Jade said. "She could even join our team!"

"Let's ask her tonight," I said.

I wrote down everything in my journal, and we came up with a timeline and a list of things we'd need to do to make the project work, and then we moved on to Trevor's idea of joining his mom at the next City Council meeting. They were going to talk about a proposal to build a new shelter in Port City. One that was right in town so people didn't have to take the bus.

"Mom says we need a big crowd there to show support," Trevor said.

"We could make flyers to spread the word," Anji offered.

"Would it help to write a letter to the newspaper?" Jade asked, and Kris jumped in with plans to get other kids from school to sign it.

I never expected to be the leader of a Real-Life Superhero team, but it turns out I'm pretty good at it. I'm organized and I pay close attention to what everyone is trying to say. Maybe that's what Kris was thinking when he nominated me for team leader. Or maybe he was just being nice. Either way, I was glad he did.

"Okay, let's talk about today. When we're out on the mission, make sure you only use your superhero names," I said. "Trevor, you still haven't told us yours."

Trevor let out a groan of agony, and Anji gaped at him.

"You *still* don't know?" she asked.

"How hard can it be?" Jade teased.

"Easy for you to say. You *stole* yours," Trevor said.

"She didn't steal it," I said. "She didn't even know about those other Nightshades."

Trevor's sparkly green mask had slipped sideways so he looked cockeyed, like an experimental art painting. He was seriously worried. Like his whole world hinged on finding the right RLSH name.

"All the good names are taken," he moaned.

"No way. You'll figure out the best one," I said, and Anji gave him a supportive pat on the shoulder.

"Your true soul name will always find you. WHEN you're ready for it."

We all swiveled our heads toward the sound of Crystal Warrior's commanding voice. Jade and Anji sucked in their breath and Trevor practically turned purple with excitement as the Reality Shifters filed in: Ocean, Papa Wheelie, Crystal Warrior, Silver Sparrow. Even Scar. They'd all come to help with our first Oceanside Optimists mission: a candy-and-care drop-off to Safe Harbor Women's Shelter.

It had taken forever to convince my parents to let us form the club. Even when they finally agreed, they had a long list of conditions. Full oversight of the schedule, participants, and mission details. No crime-fighting. No scary costumes. Mom got to personally choose the driver, who

I assumed must be Mr. Iftin, since she'd approved him to be our adviser. After making him sit through an actual job interview. Twice. Technically, Ms. Pryor was supposed to assign club advisers, but she was a good sport about it. So was Mr. Iftin.

"You guys collected all this?" Crystal Warrior motioned around the room to the boxes and bags filled with toothpaste, tampons, shampoo, candy, and other supplies we'd been gathering from our classmates.

"Six full boxes!" I said, feeling proud.

"I made something for you," Crystal said. "For your first mission."

She held out a choker that looked almost identical to the one around her own neck. Only instead of a pink star sapphire, the stone in the center was deep red with dark flecks in it.

"Blood jasper," she said. "It's a crystal to promote courage, strength, and confidence."

The stone felt cold as she clasped it around my neck and I closed my eyes, trying to feel if there was courage and confidence seeping into my skin.

"I can't feel it," I said. "How do you know if it works?"

Crystal laughed. "You've already got everything you need, Spectrum," she said in her movie-superhero voice.

"The stone is just to remind you what's inside your own heart."

I touched my fingers to the stone and I swear, I did feel something. A spark, deep down, that had been there all along.

"Excuse me! Reporter coming through."

I blushed as Dad pushed his way past all the super-heroes with his whole recording setup.

"*Dad*," I whispered. He hadn't told me he was coming. And he especially hadn't said anything about putting us on the news.

"I'm here with Zinnia Helinski, co-founder of the young-est Real-Life Superhero team in Port City," he said. "Zinnia, what inspired you to form the Oceanside Optimists?"

Dad smiled and pushed the microphone in my direction. I could feel the silence in the room as everyone waited for me to say something. My face got hotter.

"Well . . . um . . ." I took a breath and looked around at all the superheroes staring at me. "My brother, Wally, loved adventures. Or . . . he used to before he died." I paused to see how Dad would take it. Talking about Wally in front of strangers.

"He did, didn't he?" Dad's voice was soft, but he was still smiling, so I kept going.

"He liked the exciting parts," I said. "But *my* favorite part of an adventure is when you get to the darkest point and then there's a light. Like a rainbow after a storm. I know bringing people shampoo and socks and candy isn't like the biggest deal. It's probably not going to fix somebody's life . . . but it might change their day. I think Wally would've liked it. Bringing hope and adventure into the world at the same time."

There was a moment where Dad stood there holding the microphone, beaming, and my ears burned with the silence all around us. Then Papa Wheelie started to clap, and Scar gave a whoop. And then there was all this embarrassing applause before my mom, of all people, burst into the room and everyone gasped in surprise.

"Sorry I'm late!" Mom was a little sweaty, like she'd been running through the halls, and she smoothed down her Powerhouse Café apron while we all stared. "I got stuck in traffic. I was worried I was going to hold us all up. But never fear, your driver is here!"

I couldn't help it. I started to laugh. A full-on belly laugh. The kind that would have made me spit take for sure if I'd been drinking root beer. Kris and Jade and Anji laughed, too, and Trevor actually fell on the floor he was laughing so hard.

"Jen . . . *What* are you wearing?" Dad asked.

Mom lifted a hand awkwardly to her head and adjusted a giant foam hat. In the shape of a coffee cup.

"I thought it could be my superhero gimmick," she said. "The Caffeinator!"

"You're going to be an RLSH?" I asked.

"Willow talked me into it," Mom said, turning red. "I couldn't find a driver I approved of, and your Dad and Derek are so busy with their new project so . . . can I be an Oceanside Optimist?"

"Yes!" I said.

Mom tried to arrange us in a group, but it was a challenge with all the giggling. "Here, scrunch together. I promised Willow I'd take a picture. She wants you to call her later and give her all the details. What's so funny? Is the hat not right? It seemed perfect to *me*."

It felt so good. Laughing like I could bust a gut. But we had a mission to carry out. It was time to get moving. I looked to Crystal Warrior, knowing she could round everyone up and get us back on track with a snap of her fingers. But she only shook her head and smiled.

"This is your team, Spectrum," she said. "You've *got* this."

I straightened my shoulders and tested out a Crystal

Warrior–style superhero voice. A voice that was strong enough to echo through space. Deep enough to reach the ocean floor. Powerful enough to split a single wavelength of light into all the colors of the rainbow. I imagined my voice shooting an arc of color into the sky. An arc of hope. Of joy.

"Superheroes!" I said. "Circle up!"

NOTES AND ACKNOWLEDGMENTS

GRIEF

Like Zinnia, all of us will experience grief in our lives. When we lose someone we love, there are so many different emotions to process. It can be hard to understand and express how we feel, and if you are at all like me, you might find it's especially difficult to ask for help. Talking with friends, family, and others you trust is an important place to start. Art, music, and writing are also excellent tools for expressing how you feel.

I would like to offer a special thanks to Charlotte Agell for writing the picture book *Maybe Tomorrow?* I read it many times while writing this book, and each time felt like a warm hug. If you or someone you know has lost a loved one, I highly recommend it.

RLSH

My husband, Kevin, and I were listening to the audiobook of Jon Ronson's *Lost at Sea* when I first learned about the real-life RLSH movement that was popular in the early 2010s (and still exists today on a smaller scale). I was intrigued that there were people who felt so strongly that change needed to happen in the world that they would put on costumes and try to *do* something about it. I read lots of books and articles about the RLSH before creating my own imaginary teams: the Reality Shifters and the eXtreme eXamples.

The goals, efforts, and results of the RLSH teams and individuals I read about ranged broadly. Some wanted to assist people experiencing homelessness or to clean up local parks and visit children's hospitals; others wanted to set up a neighborhood watch to increase the safety of their communities; while some felt the urge to fight crime in a (frankly, dangerous) vigilante style. A small number even claimed to actually have superpowers! In my research, the RLSH I admired were the ones who were willing to listen, learn, adapt, and work with others to help create positive change in their communities.

What fascinated me the most about the worldwide RLSH community was that it was made up of individuals with an extraordinarily wide range of belief systems—religious, atheist, conservative, liberal—every ideology you can imagine. And yet, they put those differences aside to combine forces for the common good. It was an excellent reminder that we don't always have to agree with one another in order to work together. Working together is how we will make the world a safer, healthier, and happier place.

ADVOCACY

In *Not All Heroes*, Zinnia meets Derek, Pearl, Mary, and several other individuals who do not have permanent housing. There are as many different experiences around homelessness and home insecurity as there are shades of a rainbow—and the experiences depicted in this story are just a few examples. There are real-life superheroes all around us who are working in small and large ways to address the many issues that contribute to home and food insecurity. No matter what your own housing situation is, there are things you can do, too!

For instance, The Emergency Action Network (TEAN) is a group of moms in my town who noticed that too many families and children in our community were struggling to meet their most basic needs. They also knew that plenty of people would like to help. So they organized a network (kind of like a superhero team!) to make a change. When TEAN learns that a student needs school supplies, a winter coat, food, bus pass, blankets, mattresses, even socks—they put out a call for donations and find community members who can provide the needed items. Importantly, to protect the privacy of children and families receiving the donations, TEAN works with our school department to organize referrals, collect goods and services, and ensure that the items get to their intended recipients anonymously. If you'd like to learn about starting a TEAN in your community, you can visit: https://emergencyactionnetwork.com/start-a-tean-in -your-community/.

Other schools around the country have programs a lot like the Free Fashion Room that Jade suggests to the Oceanside Optimists. Your school might have a weekend backpack program or a summer lunch service that you can participate in and/or help out with.

Outside of school, many local shelters, food banks, churches, and libraries, as well as legal and policy advocacy organizations, have programs that bring volunteers together to donate time, money, and talents to help make sure *all* people have access to a place to sleep and food to eat. These groups are made up of regular people who have seen a problem and decided to do something about it—real-life superheroes! They might host events, organize letter-writing campaigns, and advocate for things like public housing, rent relief, or more mental health and addiction resources. National organizations like the United Way (unitedway.org), Feeding America (feedingamerica.org), and Operation Warm (operationwarm.org) will point you in the direction of pro-grams, events, and resources near you—as well as provide information to help you build your own advocacy programs from scratch.

It all starts with being curious, paying attention, listening, and educating yourself. A great place to find learning resources about home insecurity and many other social justice issues is Teaching Tolerance (tolerance.org). If we can understand *why* inequities exist, then we can start to figure out how we can work together to build change.

MY TEAM

Writing a book is a lot easier when you have a team of superheroes to help you get the job done. So many people contributed to this project—some helped me brainstorm, edit, organize my life, and think around corners; others used their expertise to turn my manuscript into a beautifully designed book and helped it find its way in the world; and still others offered moral support, flexibility, and kindness (and watched lots of superhero movies with me). I am indebted to the readers who advised me on depictions of homelessness and food insecurity, as well as to those who gave advice on scenes involving disability, advocacy, policing, cancer, and grief. Every day, I am overwhelmed with gratitude for my team.

On my personal Superhero Roster for *Not All Heroes*:

Val, Dave, Kim, Trevor, Ruby, Gavin, Kerry, Tom, Albert, Jonny.

Anna, Bethye, Ashton, Brian.

Kevin. And the Honey Gang.

CJ, Eli, Reba, Bill.

Shalini, Veena, Scott.

The Beetons, Danyon, Andrea.

Michele, Jim, Rick, Jennifer, Kevin.

Katelyn Pratt.

Lydia Sigwarth.

Debbi Michiko Florence, Ann Braden, Cynthia Lord, Kate Egan.

My generous, flexible, and creative music students and their families.

John Cusick and the Folio Superhero Team.

Grace Kendall, Elizabeth Lee, Cassie Gonzales, Brittany Pearlman, Allyson Floridia, Mallory Grigg, and the brilliant minds at MacKids and FSG.

Maike Plenzke.

Kevin.

Did I mention Kevin? Because I *really* couldn't have written this without him.

Deepest thanks to my readers for all the light you shine in the world.

CHECK OUT MORE ADVENTURES WITH A TOUCH OF MAGIC AND MYSTERY FROM JOSEPHINE CAMERON!

Best friends come in all shapes, sizes, and . . . scales?

• An Amazon Best Book of the Month •

"An offbeat, earnest novel for those who believe in magic, and those who wish they did." —*Booklist*

Also available in paperback!

When a bejeweled dog collar goes missing, Epic McDade has to sniff out the thief before summer ends.

• A *Parents* magazine Storytime Pick •

★ "Short chapters and a breathless pace make this a clever, engrossing, plot-driven tale with plenty of unusual, well-developed characters—even the dogs . . . Thoroughly entertaining— mystery fans and dog lovers will lap this one up." —*Kirkus Reviews*, starred review